THE FRAGRANT FLOWER

The mildness and beauty of Hong Kong were so welcome after the horrible English winters. As lovely and delicate as the flower she was named for, Azalea needed warmth and sunlight to survive.

Not that Azalea would ever be truly happy in her new home. Her aunt and uncle kept her in a humiliating state of domestic slavery. Her inferior position, they insisted, was more than justified by the unmentionable disgrace in her past.

Her vicious guardians had succeeded in breaking Azalea's spirit. But they couldn't prevent a determined young man from falling in love with her. Nor could they stop him from uncovering the shameful secret that clouded Azalea's happiness.

BARBARA CARTLAND

Bantam Books by Barbara Cartland
Ask your bookseller for the books you have missed

Barbara Cartland
The Fragrant Flower

THE FRAGRANT FLOWER
A Bantam Book / March 1976

Published simultaneously in the United States and Canada

Bantam Books are published by Bantam Books, Inc. Its trade-
mark, consisting of the words "Bantam Books" and the por-
trayal of a bantam, is registered in the United States Patent
Office and in other countries. Marca Registrada. Bantam
Books, Inc., 666 Fifth Avenue, New York, New York 10019.

PRINTED IN THE UNITED STATES OF AMERICA

This book is dedicated to my friends in Hong Kong, and especially to George Wright Nooth, for many years Deputy Chief of Police, who showed me the New Territories and took me to the Red Chinese border.

To the Mandarin Hotel, which in my opinion is not only the most glamorous in the world but also has the best service, and to their sweet, delightful Assistant to the General Manager, Miss Kai-Yin Lo, who introduced me to her charming family and the superlative Chinese food one finds only in a private house.

Author's Note

The controversy over the Regimental Band was a burning problem in Hong Kong in 1880. The descriptions of the poisoning of the bread and the way thieves used the storm-water drains are all authentic.

An exhaustive report on the origin and characteristics of Chinese slavery and domestic servitude in Hong Kong was reviewed in a debate in the House of Lords on June 21, 1880.

It was stated that the Attorney General had been wrong in his exposition of the law, but that, on the other hand, the Chief Justice had rushed into wild exaggerations.

Sir John Pope-Hennessy was the first Governor of Hong Kong who treated the Chinese as partners. He took the first steps to translate into reality the ideal of nondiscrimination between the races which had appeared on the Governor's instructions in 1886 and in British Colonial Policy much earlier.

In this enlightened attitude he was in advance of his time but he was, however, a poor administrator and an impossible man to work with. He quarrelled with all his officials and was distrusted by the Colonial Office.

He left Hong Kong in March 1882 for the Governorship of Mauritius, where again he aroused intense hostility. He had the right ideas but went about them in the wrong way.

Chapter One

1880

"There, Miss Azalea, I've finished the Master's sandwiches and now I'll see if I can find Burrows to take them along to him."

"Do not worry, Mrs. Burrows," Azalea replied. "I will take them. Sit down and rest your legs."

"I don't mind telling you, Miss Azalea, my legs feel as if they don't belong to me, and me back's broken in two places."

"Do sit down!" Azalea begged. "It has been too much for you!"

That, she knew, was the truth, but it would have been useless to tell her Aunt so.

It seemed to Azalea real cruelty to have made an aged couple like the Burrowses undertake a party that her Uncle, General Sir Frederick Osmund, and his wife were giving before they left England.

The Burrowses were now very old and had served the General's father until his death. Then they had lived in the house in Hampstead as caretakers, and Azalea was sure they had not expected to be required to go on working at their age.

But the General, with his wife, twin daughters, and his niece, had moved into Battlesdon House for two months before leaving for Hong Kong.

Although a number of extra servants had been engaged, it was the Butler, Burrows, who coped with cheap, untrained footmen in the front of the house, while Mrs. Burrows, who was nearly eighty, did the cooking.

Used to Indian servants who obeyed their slightest
wish and cost very little either in wages or food, Lady
Osmund had made no effort to adjust herself to English
conditions.

When the General had been at Camberley it had
been easier, because he had soldier-servants who attended to him, and wives from the married quarters
who were only too glad to earn some extra money.

But in London, because Lady Osmund was cheese-
paring when it came to wages, they could engage only
the youngest and most inexperienced girls, who, as
Mrs. Burrows said over and over again, were more
trouble than help.

It was inevitable, Azalea thought when the party
was proposed, that she, who had made out the lists and
sent out the invitations, should be relegated to the
kitchen.

"Mrs. Burrows will never manage, Aunt Emily," she
had said to Lady Osmund. "The new kitchen-maid is
really half-witted and I think the scullery-maid should
be in an asylum.

"The two daily-women will come and help with the
washing-up," Lady Osmund replied.

"There is all the cooking for the dinner-party and
for the supper later at the Ball," Azalea pointed out.

There was a pause. Then, with an unpleasant look in
her eyes which Azalea knew only too well, Lady Osmund said:

"As you are so anxious about Mrs. Burrows, I am
sure you would wish to help her, Azalea."

After a short silence Azalea asked in a small voice:

"You do not wish me to be ... present at the ...
Ball, Auntie Emily?"

"I consider it quite unnecessary for you to appear on
such an occasion," Lady Osmund replied. "I thought
your Uncle had made it clear to you what your position in this house should be, and you will continue to
keep your place, Azalea, after we reach Hong Kong."

Azalea did not reply, but she was conscious of a
sense of shock that her Aunt should express her dislike
so forcibly. After two years' experience she had come

to expect the treatment she received, but it still had the power to hurt her.

Nevertheless she bit back the protest which came to her lips, for the simple reason that she had been afraid, or rather terrified, when she learnt of her Uncle's appointment to Hong Kong, that they would not take her with them.

She longed with a yearning that was inexpressible to be in the East again; to feel the sunshine; to hear the soft sing-song voices; to smell on the air the fragrance of the flowers and spices, dust and woodsmoke; most of all to know that she was no longer shivering from the cold of England.

Hong Kong would not be the same as India, but it was East of Suez, and as such was permeated in Azalea's mind with the golden glow of a sunlit Paradise.

It seemed more like a century than only two years since she had been sent home from India, stunned into an inarticulate misery at her father's death and the events which followed it.

She had been so happy with him, looking after him after her mother's death, acting as hostess for him in the Army bungalows he was allotted in the various parts of the country in which the Regiment was stationed.

When they had gone to the North-West Provinces Azalea had been thrilled, even though it meant that her father often had to leave her alone for months on end when he was serving on the Frontier and there was trouble amongst the tribesmen.

When things were quiet she was able to accompany him. But when, as so often happened, women were excluded and sent back to a safe base, she was still content because she was with soldier-servants who had served her father and mother for many years.

There were also wives and mothers of other Officers in the Regiment ready to take pity on what they thought was her loneliness.

Azalea did not say so because she was too tactful, but in fact she was never lonely.

She loved India—she loved everything about it, and her days seemed to be full with all she wanted to learn; the lessons she arranged for herself with various different teachers, and self-imposed tasks she performed in whatever bungalow she and her father occupied.

She had of course met her father's much older and most distinguished brother, General Sir Frederick, on various occasions, and she had thought both him and his wife to be stiff and pompous.

It was only later that she was to learn how little they had in common and find that her Uncle's character and personality in no way resembled her adored father's.

Derek Osmund had always been gay and carefree except as far as his Regimental duties were concerned.

He enjoyed life and he made everyone round him enjoy it too, and yet there was nothing raffish about his gaiety.

He was a great humanitarian, and Azalea could not remember a time when he had not been concerned with the sufferings of some unfortunate family.

Often when he returned from the parade-ground there would be half a dozen Indians waiting for him, some with cuts and bruises, others with eye complaints, festering sores, or sick babies.

He had little medical training, but his sympathy, his understanding, and the manner in which he laughed at their fears and gave them new hope for the future sent them away happy as no Doctor was able to do.

"He made it all such fun!" Azalea would often remind herself.

It was something her mother had said over and over again in the years when they had all been together.

"Papa has a holiday," she would say to Azalea. "Now we can have some fun together! What about a picnic?"

Then they would all three ride off to picnic beside a river, on the top of a hill, or in some ancient cave which would turn out to be part of the history of India.

Looking back on her childhood, Azalea would feel there had never been a day when the sun was not shining; never a night when she had not gone to sleep with a smile on her lips.

Then suddenly, out of the blue, had come disaster!

"How could it happen? Oh, God, how could You let it happen?" Azalea had cried wildly into the night on the ship which carried her away from India to the cold and what seemed to her the impenetrable darkness of England.

Even now she could hardly believe that it was not part of some terrible nightmare and she would not wake to find that the two years she had spent with her Uncle and Aunt had just been a part of her imagination.

But it was true: true that her father was dead, and that living in her Uncle's house she was treated like a *pariah!*

She was despised, disliked, and humiliated in every possible way because the General would never forgive his younger brother for the way in which he had died.

"Papa was right! He was absolutely right!" Azalea would say to herself.

Sometimes she would long to scream the same words at her Uncle as he sat at the end of the table looking incredibly self-satisfied, and yet speaking to her in tones that, she told herself, she would not have used to a dog.

She learnt what she must expect in the future when they arrived back in England and her Uncle talked to her in his Study.

The journey home had been an inexpressible torture of misery and physical discomfort.

It was November and the storm in the Bay of Biscay left most people on board ship prostrate.

But it was not the buffeting of the wind or the pitching and tossing of the ship which Azalea minded, but the fact that she was so cold.

In the years she had lived in India she had become acclimatised to the excessive heat, and perhaps the Russian blood in her veins had prevented her from finding the hot, stifling air of the plains as exhausting as did the pure-bred English.

Her mother had been of Russian origin and born in India, which, Azalea learnt, was another sin for which she must be punished because her Uncle did not care for foreigners and despised Anglo-Indians.

There was, however, little of her mother's dark-eyed beauty and exquisite bone-structure to be seen when Azalea, thin to the point of ugliness, stood in front of her Uncle and thought that her teeth must chatter aloud because the Study was so cold.

Her unhappiness at her father's death had prevented her from eating enough on board ship, her eyes were swollen from weeping, and her dark hair, which in India had seemed to glow with strange lights, was lank and lifeless.

She looked miserable and immature, and her appearance did nothing to soften the hardness of her Uncle's eyes, or the note of dislike she could hear so clearly in his voice.

"You and I, Azalea," he said, "are both aware that your father's reprehensible and shameless behaviour could have brought disgrace upon our family name."

"Papa did what was right!" Azalea murmured.

"Right?" the General ejaculated with a sound like a pistol-shot. "Right to kill a superior Officer—to murder him?"

"You know that Papa did not mean to kill the Colonel," Azalea said defensively, "it was an accident! But he did try to prevent the Colonel, who was quite mad, from brutally ill-treating a woman."

"A native!" the General said contemptuously. "Doubtless she deserved the beating the Colonel was giving her."

"She was not the first woman he had treated in such a way," Azalea retorted. "Everyone knew of the Colonel's perverted cruelty."

Her voice vibrated with the horror of what she remembered.

But how could she explain to this stern, granite-like figure in front of her what it had meant to hear a woman's screams ringing out from the Colonel's bungalow, her shrieks turning the soft, dark loveliness of the night into something hideous and bestial?

Derek Osmund had stood it for some time. Then as the screams seemed to grow more insistent he had jumped to his feet.

"Damnit all!" he exclaimed. "This cannot go on! It is intolerable! That girl is little more than a child, and the daughter of our *dhirzi*."

It was then that Azalea had realised who was screaming. She was a girl of perhaps thirteen who came with her father, who was a tailor, to work on the verandah of the bungalow, assisting him with his stitching and cutting.

She was almost as experienced as he was in making up a gown in under twenty-four hours, mending an Officer's uniform, or fashioning a new shirt.

Azalea had often talked with the girl, thinking how pretty she was with her long, dark eye-lashes and gentle eyes.

She always pulled her sari across her face whenever a man approached, but the Colonel, even though he was usually the worse for drink, must have seen the delicacy of that oval face and the sweetly curved breasts which the sari could not conceal.

Derek Osmund had gone to the Colonel's bungalow.

There had been a cessation of the screams, then the Colonel's voice raised in anger, and another scream, followed by silence.

It was only later that Azalea was able to piece together what had happened.

Her father had found the *dhirzi's* daughter half naked, being thrashed by the Colonel as if she were an animal.

It was a prelude to raping the girl, known to his junior Officers as the method he used to satisfy his desires.

"What the devil do you want?" the Colonel had asked as Derek Osmund appeared.

"You cannot treat a woman in such a way, Sir!"

"Are you giving me orders, Osmund?" the Colonel demanded.

"I am simply telling you, Sir, that your behaviour is both inhuman and a bad example to the men."

The Colonel glared at him.

"Get out of my bungalow and mind your own damned business!" he shouted.

"It is my business," Derek Osmund answered. "It is the business of every decent man to prevent such cruelty."

The Colonel had laughed and it was an ugly sound.

"Get the hell out of here," he commanded, "unless you prefer to watch!"

He tightened his hold on the cane he held in his hand and reached out to take the loosened hair of the Indian girl in the other and drag her to her knees.

Her back was already a mess of weals from the beating she had received, and as the cane fell again she screamed; but it was a weak effort and it was obvious that her strength was nearly spent.

It was then that Derek Osmund had struck the Colonel.

His fist caught him on the chin, and the Colonel, who had drunk a great deal at dinner and was not particularly steady on his feet, fell backwards, hitting the back of his head on a large wrought-iron pedestal which stood at the side of the room.

For a younger and less debauched man with a stronger heart the fall would not have been fatal, but when the Regimental Surgeon was summoned to the bungalow he pronounced the Colonel dead.

After that Azalea was not certain what happened, except that the Surgeon fetched Sir Frederick, who happened to be staying with the Governor of the Province at Government House, which was only a short distance from the Camp.

Sir Frederick, taking command of the situation, talked to his brother, who did not return to his own bungalow.

The following morning he was found dead outside the Camp and Azalea was told that there had been an unfortunate accident when her father was pursuing a wild animal.

Had he not shot himself, Azalea realised, there would have been a Military Court-Martial, while inevitably the death of the Colonel would have been brought before the Civil Courts.

As it was, the Regimental Surgeon gave out that he had informed the Colonel that his heart was in bad state and any exertion might prove fatal.

With the exception of Sir Frederick, the Surgeon, and one senior Officer in the Regiment, no-one knew exactly what had occurred, except of course Azalea.

"Your father's outrageous behaviour could have brought disgrace upon his family, his Regiment, and his country," the General said now. "That is why, Azalea, you will never speak of it to anyone in the whole of your life. Is that clear?"

There was silence. Then after a moment Azalea said in a low voice:

"I would not, of course, wish to talk about it to an outsider, but I imagine that one day, when I marry, my husband would wish to learn the truth."

"You will never marry!"

The words were a plain statement.

Azalea looked at her Uncle wide-eyed.

"Why should I never marry?" she asked.

"Because, as your Guardian, I would not give my permission for you to do so," the General answered. "You must pay the price of your father's sins, and what happened in India you will take to your grave with sealed lips."

For a moment the full meaning of what he had said hardly penetrated Azalea's mind. Then he added contemptuously:

"As you are singularly unattractive, it is unlikely that any man would wish to marry you. However, if anyone should be so misguided as to offer for your hand, the answer will be no!"

Azalea had drawn in her breath and for the moment she could find no words with which to speak.

This was something she had never anticipated, had never thought would occur in her life.

She was only sixteen and therefore her heart was not

engaged in any way, yet vaguely she had always thought that one day she would marry and have children; and that perhaps she would continue in her married life to be part of the Regiment.

She had grown up in the shadow of it, proud of what it meant to her father and to the men he inspired with his leadership and who loved him because he cared for them.

It was interwoven in her thoughts and in everything she did; the horses, the parades, the times when the soldiers moved station with their guns, their baggage-wagons, their wives and families, and the innumerable army of "hangers-on" who seemed as much a part of the Regiment as the Sepoys themselves.

She would wake in the morning to the sound of Reveille and she would hear "The Last Post" echoing amongst the cantonments as dusk came and the flag was lowered on the flag-pole.

The Regiment was her home, a part of her life, and when she thought of the pennants fluttering from the lances of the Cavalry or the men whistling as they went about their work, she would find that the ache that had been permanently within her since the death of her father was intensified.

'One day,' she had thought to herself as she left India, 'I shall go back. I shall be with them again.'

Now her Uncle was telling her that there was to be nothing in her future except to wait upon her Aunt and be reproved or abused a dozen times a day.

It was not only her father's crime for which she was beng punished. Both her Uncle and Aunt made it very clear how much they had disliked her mother because she was Russian.

"You will not mention your mother's ancestry to anyone," Sir Frederick admonished Azalea. "It was an extremely unfortunate choice at the time your father married, and I expressed my disapproval very clearly."

"Why do you disapprove?" Azalea enquired.

"Because a mixture of races is never desirable, and Russians are not even Europeans! Your father should have taken a decent English girl as his wife."

"Are you implying that my mother was not decent?" Azalea asked angrily.

Sir Frederick's lips tightened.

"As your mother is dead, I will not express my opinion of her. All I will say is that you will keep silent concerning her Russian origin."

The General's voice sharpened as he continued:

"At any moment we may be again at war with Russia, this time on the North-West Frontier. Even without open hostilities they stir up the tribesmen, infiltrate our lines, and their spies are everywhere."

He looked contemptuously at Azalea's pale face and added harshly:

"I am ashamed that I must house and support anyone with their poisonous, treacherous blood in their veins! You will never mention your mother's name while you are under my protection."

At first Azalea had been too miserable to realise what was happening to her. Then after a year, when she was no longer permitted to continue with her education, she found that she was little more than a drudge and an extra servant.

At seventeen, when her first cousins, Violet and Daisy, the twins, were excited about making their debut and going to Balls, she had become lady's-maid, seamstress, secretary, house-keeper, and jack-of-all trades.

Now, at eighteen, she felt as if she had spent her whole life as a domestic servant and there was nothing to look forward to, except years and years of attending to the same chores, day in and day out.

Then like a miracle out of the sky had come the news that the General's command at Aldershot was over and he was to be posted to Hong Kong.

Azalea could hardly believe it. And at first she was quite certain that they would leave her behind.

But she guessed that they were concerned to keep her under their eye; for the stigma of her father's death was still to the General a menacing secret which he was afraid she might expose.

It was this, she knew, and the memory of her

mother which made them keep her out of sight of their
social friends.

They could not deny that she was their niece, but
they told everyone that she was shy and retiring.

"Azalea is not interested in parties or dances," she
heard her Aunt say to a friend who had tentatively
suggested she should be included in an invitation extended to her cousins.

She longed to cry out that this was untrue, but she
knew that to do so would only bring down her Uncle's
wrath upon her and her position would remain exactly
the same.

But at least in Hong Kong she would be nearer to
her beloved India. At least there would be sunshine,
flowers and birds, and people would smile at her.

"If you are going to be kind enough, Miss Azalea, to
take the sandwiches along to the Library," Mrs. Burrows said, interrupting Azalea's thoughts, "there's a decanter of whisky waiting in the pantry. The General
said we were not to put it out until the party was
nearly over, otherwise the guests might drink it. You
know, he likes to keep his whisky to himself!"

"Yes, I know," Azalea said, "and I will take it along
too. I am sure Burrows is feeling the rheumatism in his
legs by now and I do not want to give him any more to
do."

"You're real kind, Miss Azalea, that's what you are!
I don't know how I'd have got through the dinner or
the supper without your help."

That was true enough.

Azalea, who had now become quite an experienced
cook, was responsible for nearly all the supper-dishes
and half of those that had been served at dinner.

"Well, I am glad it is over!" she said aloud as she
picked up the plate of sandwiches neatly decorated
with parsley. "I will have a cup of tea with you, Mrs.
Burrows, when I get back."

"You deserve it, Miss Azalea," Mrs. Burrows replied.

Azalea went from the large, high-ceilinged kitchen

with its flagged floor that was very tiring to stand on, along the passage to the pantry.

Old Burrows had left the square-cut glass decanter filled with the General's whisky on a side-table.

It was standing on a silver salver and Azalea put the sandwiches beside it and lifted the tray with both hands.

She could hear in the distance the sound of music coming from the big Drawing-Room that had been cleared for the dancing.

It was a large, attractive room with French windows opening onto the garden, which, as it was winter, were closed.

But Azalea could imagine how attractive it could be during the summer when it was warm enough to walk from the gas-lit room into the fragrant garden which seemed to her to be on the very top of London.

She could look from the windows down into the green valley which Constable had painted in many of his pictures.

But it was in fact the garden which interested her because she knew the General's father had been a famous gardener and after leaving the Army had spent his retirement in making it not only beautiful but also famous among horticulturlists.

He had managed to grow many new and exotic plants and flowers which had not been seen in England before and which he had obtained from all over the world.

It was his obsession with flowers which had made Colonel Osmund decree that his granddaughters should all be christened with the name of a flower.

"It is typical," Lady Osmund had said acidly, "that your mother should have chosen such a singularly inappropriate name for you."

Azalea longed to retort that she thought both "Violet" and "Daisy" were commonplace and rather dull, but she learnt after a few months of living with her Aunt that it was very unwise to answer back.

Her Aunt did not beat her, although Azalea was quite certain that she would have liked to do so; but she had a habit of slapping and pinching which could be very painful.

She was a large, overpowering woman, while Azalea was small and delicately made, and it was obvious who would come off the better in any physical contest.

After having her face slapped until her cheeks were on fire and her arms pinched until the bruises were purple against her skin, Azalea did her best not to antagonise her Aunt.

Now, hurrying along the passage which led to the Library and carrying the sandwiches and drink which constituted the General's invariable night-cap, Azalea wondered what it would have been like if she could have had a new gown and attended her Uncle's party.

She knew from the invitations that only a small number of younger guests had been invited, and those were in fact either Officers or the sons and daughters of families which her Aunt considered of social importance.

"If I had been having a party," Azalea told herself, "I would want to ask my friends . . . my real friends."

Then she remembered that she was never likely to have any.

She entered the Study which was at the opposite end of the house from the other Reception Rooms and saw that the fire was burning brightly in the grate, which meant that Burrows must have remembered to make it up.

The gas-light gave out a mellow glow which hid the shabbiness of the arm-chairs and the parts of the carpet which were worn with age.

But there were books all round the room and Azalea, although she had very little time, had already sneaked a number of them away upstairs to her bedroom and read them with joy.

It was however hard, in the house in Hampstead, to read late into the night because her bed-room was so cold.

Violet and Daisy, like her Aunt, had fires in their rooms, lit by an under-housemaid first thing in the morning, and kept burning throughout the day.

But Azalea was not accorded such a privilege, and no amount of blankets could keep her from shivering and her nose from turning blue and pinched even with the windows closed.

She put the whisky and sandwiches down on a table and turned towards the fire, holding out her hands to the blaze.

As she did so she saw the reflection of herself in the mirror which hung over the mantelpiece.

Her appearance had altered in the last two years: her breasts were still a little immature, but her bones no longer stood out sharply.

Her face was heart-shaped, very like her mother's, and her eyes seemed to have grown larger so that they were arresting the moment anyone looked at her.

If she was unusually pale it was because she was overworked and seldom had an opportunity to go outside the house. Not that she wished to brave the winter winds and the cold of Hampstead Heath.

Azalea looked at herself carefully.

She did not know if her dark hair and big worried eyes were attractive or not.

She only wished her father was there to tell her what he thought. Then she looked away from her face and down at the enveloping apron in which she had been cooking all day.

Underneath it she wore a gown which had belonged either to Violet or to Daisy. They were always dressed in identical fashion and she knew that while it was becoming to them because they looked their best in pale pastel shades of blue, pink, and beige, such colours were to her unbecoming.

She did not quite know why. Perhaps it was because by the time she received the gowns they were worn out, faded with washing, and often difficult to adjust to her figure.

"Oh well, who is likely to see me?" she asked of her reflection, then as she spoke the words aloud she heard footsteps approaching the door.

She knew it was unlikely to be her Uncle since he could not leave his guests, and as she had no wish to encounter strangers she slipped hurriedly behind the heavy velvet curtains which covered the window.

She had hardly had time to conceal herself before the door opened.

"There is no-one here," a man said in a deep voice. "Let us sit down for a moment, George. We have done our duty in no uncertain fashion!"

"*You* have, Mirvin," was the answer.

Having written out the invitations, Azalea was now aware of who both the men were.

There was only one man on the list with the unusual name of Mirvin, and that was Lord Sheldon, who on accepting had asked if he might bring with him a friend, Captain George Widcombe, who was staying with him.

Azalea was well aware that Lady Osmund, being so delighted at the thought of Lord Sheldon attending the party, would have agreed to any suggestion he might make.

The General had suggested that he should be sent an invitation since, as he informed his wife, Lord Sheldon before he came into the title had served in the Seventeenth Hussars and he had known him in India.

"A clever young man," he had said grudgingly, "but I never cared for him personally. However, the Colonel secretly thinks a lot of him and he is visiting Hong Kong."

"Will he be there with us?" Lady Osmund had asked with a glint of interest in her hard eyes.

"He will," the General had replied briefly, and Azalea had known that for some reason her Uncle was not pleased at the idea.

Now she heard Captain Widcombe say:

"How on earth you, Mirvin, with your mantelpiece overflowing with invitations to really slap-up parties, can come to this dreary parochial show, I do not know!"

"You have not yet heard the worst of it, George," Lord Sheldon replied.

"Can there be a worse?" Captain Widcombe asked. "I see some whisky. Let us have a drink. The Champagne was appalling!"

"Army rations, dear boy! Generals always do one on the cheap!"

"That I can well believe!" Captain Widcombe replied. "Although as a matter of fact in the Guards we are rather particular!"

"Do not be such a snob, George!" Lord Sheldon remarked. "But I must admit to preferring *Aqua Vitae* to the type of fizzy muck we have been offered this evening."

"Well I must say, I think it is too bad of you, Mirvin, the first night I arrive in London to bring me here!" Captain Widcombe complained.

"I wanted you to realise what I will have to put up with on the voyage to Hong Kong."

"Good God, Mirvin! You do not mean to say you are travelling with this lot?"

"You would hardly believe it, but the Commander-in-Chief button-holed me and said that, as the General is travelling in a Troop Ship and I am booked on the *Orissa*, he would be extremely grateful if I would look after Lady Osmund and her daughters! What could I reply?"

"My dear Mirvin, having seen the lady in question, I must offer you my deepest and most sincere condolences!"

"I was hoping for a quiet voyage," Lord Sheldon went on bitterly. "I have a lot of work to do, George, and now this has been thrust upon me."

"Why on earth should the G.O.C. bother you?"

"He knows why the Colonial Office has asked me to visit Hong Kong, and the General is one of his 'blue-eyed boys.' As a matter of fact, that is why he has been given the command."

"And if he jumped at the job," Captain Widcombe said shrewdly, "I am sure it was because Her Ladyship thought it an excellent opportunity to foist those nit-witted pink-and-white twins on an unsuspecting Colony!"

"Her Ladyship has already cross-questioned me as to the social amenities she is likely to find there for her little ones."

"I suppose by that she means what sort of eligible bachelors they will encounter!" Captain Widcombe observed.

"Of course!" Lord Sheldon agreed. "What interests any Regimental mother except unattached Subalterns?"

"The Fishing Fleet!" Captain Widcombe remarked scathingly.

"Exactly! At the same time, make no mistake, George, I have seen these young women from England in action: they do not fish! They grab—they claw—they devour!"

He gave a short, disdainful laugh.

"They are man-eating tiger-cubs, every single one of them, and all I can tell you is that my heart bleeds for every fresh-faced Subaltern who finds himself shanghaied up the aisle by one of these simpering creatures and is then tied to her for the rest of his life!"

"You certainly do not paint a very pleasant picture, Mirvin!"

"I have seen too much of it," Lord Sheldon replied. "You have not yet served abroad, my dear boy, although it looks as though you will be in India before long, facing the Russians."

"Do you think there will be a war?" Captain Widcombe asked.

"I think it may be avoided," Lord Sheldon answered, "but the powers-that-be are apprehensive. They are increasing our strength in Hong Kong in case the Chinese get nasty while we are otherwise engaged."

"So that is why you are going there!"

"I wish that were the only reason!"

"What else?"

"You will hardly believe it if I tell you," Lord Sheldon replied, "but the main trouble in Hong Kong at the moment is purely domestic drama!"

"What do you mean?"

"There is a ridiculous, absurd squabble taking place between the Army, that is to say the Hong Kong Garrison under the command of General Donovan, and the Governor."

He paused before he continued:

"It is petty and completely childish but it has assumed such proportions that I have been sent out with instructions jointly from the Colonial Office and the War Office to put both the contestants in their respective corners and tell them to behave themselves!"

Captain Widcombe threw back his head and laughed.

"I do not believe it! Good God, Mirvin, after all your achievements and all your brilliance in really dangerous situations, I can hardly see you playing Nanny!"

"And acting as a kind of Cooks' Courier to Lady Osmund and her man-hunting twins on the way out!" Lord Sheldon added bitterly.

"What is the Governor of Hong Kong like?" Captain Widcombe asked in a more serious tone.

"His name is Pope-Hennessey. He has just been knighted. He is apparently extremely tactless and has caused General Donovan to send dozens of complaints about him back to the War Office."

Lord Sheldon gave a short laugh with no humour in it.

"You will hardly believe this, George, but things have been brought to explosion point by the fact that on May twenty-sixth, which is the Queen's Birthday, it is traditional for the Garrison Band to be detailed to play at Government House."

"Sounds reasonable to me!" Captain Widcombe exclaimed.

"That is what it may sound," Lord Sheldon agreed. "But General Donovan has refused point-blank to release the Band and has arranged an alternative Queen's Birthday-dinner at the barracks!"

Captain Widcombe laughed uproariously.

"I do not believe it! And they have sent for you to solve this difficult and dangerous problem!"

"There is more to it than that," Lord Sheldon said drily. "Sir John Pope-Hennessey has what is called locally a 'Chinese Policy.' He has reformed the prisons and abandoned public floggings and branding on the necks of criminals."

"That must have caused a commotion," Captain Widcombe exclaimed.

"It has!" his friend agreed. "What is more, he has given permission for the Chinese to build where they wish, and—more explosive than anything else—he actually invites Indians, Malayans, and Chinese to his of official entertainments and has made personal friends amongst them!"

"Good Lord!" Captain Widcombe exclaimed. "I see you have a social revolution on your hands!"

"Something very like it," Lord Sheldon agreed. "But you do see my difficulties?"

"And what does the War Office think?"

"Need you ask?" Lord Sheldon replied. "The natives must be kept in their place at all costs. We must show our white superiority or God knows where it will all end!"

"Well, all I can say is, I do not envy you!" Captain Widcombe exclaimed. "Give me the responsibility of guarding Buckingham Palace and you can keep the whole of the East as far as I am concerned!"

"You are insular, George, that is what is wrong with you!" Lord Sheldon answered. "It would do you good to take up the white man's burden in some far-flung outpost of the Empire. It might even broaden your mind—if you survived the experience!"

"It is an experience I have no intention of trying—unless it is forced upon me!" Captain Widcombe remarked.

Listening, Azalea heard him rise to his feet.

"Come on, Mirvin, let us leave this mausoleum and go and enjoy ourselves. I learnt in the Club of a new place where they have the prettiest and most delectable little 'soiled doves.' Many of them, I hear, are French, and to my mind they are always gayer and more amusing than the English variety."

"I will take your word for it," Lord Sheldon answered. "Personally, I am going home. I have a great deal of work to do. I cannot waste my time chasing pretty Cyprians, however attractive you make them sound!"

"The trouble with you, Mirvin, is that you are growing serious! If you are not careful you will find yourself being walked up the aisle by a milk-faced creature who is still wet behind the ears!"

"That is one thought you can dismiss from your impertient mind!" Lord Sheldon replied. "I have no intention of getting married, George, and as you are well aware, having been my friend for many years, I like picking flowers when they are in bloom!"

"And the flower I saw you with last time I was in London," Captain Widcombe said, "was an exquisitely rare bloom, and I do not suppose there was a single man in the restaurant who did not envy you!"

"Thank you!" Lord Sheldon replied. "I am glad that you approve my taste, George."

"No-one has ever questioned that it is impeccable!" Captain Widcombe laughed.

Azalea heard the two gentlemen put down their glasses and make towards the door.

She was glad that they were leaving. She had stood for a little while behind the curtain and then because she was tired she had lowered herself very gingerly to the floor.

As she did so she made a very slight noise with her foot on the uncarpeted boards in front of the window.

She had held her breath, but there had been no pause in the conversation and she was quite certain it had passed unnoticed.

Now she waited breathlessly until she heard the door close.

Rising to her feet, conscious that the draught through the window or the March wind which was whistling round the house had left her chilled, she pulled aside the curtain, intending to go and warm herself before the fire.

As she did so she stood transfixed.

One of the gentlemen was still in the Study, standing with his back to the door!

He was looking at her and she was quite certain that it was Lord Sheldon who stood there!

Just for a moment she felt unable to move, then as

her eyes, wide and frightened, were on his, he moved towards her, saying:

"I hope what you overheard, my little eavesdropper, was of use to you? Would it be impertinent to enquire why you were so interested?"

Azalea drew in her breath and moved from the window so that the curtains fell to, behind her.

"I ... I did not ... mean to ... eavesdrop," she said. "I just ... hid when I heard you ... come in."

"Why?"

The question was sharp.

"I did not wish you to ... see me."

"For any particular reason?"

Azalea made a little gesture with her hands.

"I was not dressed for a party."

"No, that is obvious," Lord Sheldon said, looking down at her apron. "What is your position here?"

Azalea did not answer and after a moment he said:

"You sound a little too cultured for a house-maid. You are too young to be the house-keeper. Perhaps you are a companion who is giving an extra hand because there is a party?"

Again Azalea did not reply and he said:

"You may think I am inquisitive, but I assure you that it is my job to be suspicious of people, especially attractive young women who listen to conversations that should not be overheard and hide themselves behind curtains!"

Azalea did not speak and with his eyes on her face he went on:

"You do not look English. What nationality are you?"

The way he spoke and the searching manner in which he looked down at her face made Azalea know that he suspected her of having an ulterior motive for listening to what he had said to his friend.

Then she told herself that he had no right to question her.

"I assure you, My Lord," she said quietly, "I am not interested in anything you have said."

"How can I be sure of that?" Lord Sheldon enquired.

"You could perhaps believe what I have . . . told you."

"I could do that," he replied. "At the same time, I may have been somewhat unguarded in what was an entirely private conversation. In which case I am of course interested in your reaction."

There was something in the way he spoke which annoyed Azalea.

He was making a mountain out of a mole-hill. Granted, it had been reprehensible of her to hide herself and listen to what he was saying. At the same time, she thought that, if he had behaved in a gentlemanly manner, he could simply have laughed it off and told her it was of little consequence.

She saw that he was better-looking and more overpowering than she had thought he would be when she listened to him from behind the curtain.

There was something too in the expression in his grey eyes which was disconcerting, and he aroused in her a strange antagonism that she had never felt before where a man was concerned.

With a proud movement she put up her chin.

"Are you really interested?"

It was a challenge and, as if he recognised it as such Lord Sheldon replied insistently:

"But of course! Are you frank—or brave—enough to tell me the truth?"

He could not have said anything which would have annoyed Azalea more.

She prided herself on her bravery and without thinking she answered:

"Very well then. I will tell you. I think that the remarks you made about women show you to be insufferably, bumptiously conceited! Those which concerned Hong Kong are just what I would expect from a hidebound Englishman who believes that the only way to assert his supremacy is to trample underfoot those who have been conquered by force of arms!"

She saw the surprise her words evoked reflected in

His Lordship's face. But regardless of the consequences, she continued:

"Do you ever think it might be a change for the better if we as a Nation behaved with kindness, consideration, and clemency to people in foreign lands?"

She drew in her breath and said:

"I have been reading about Hong Kong and I have learnt that three years ago Lord Ronald Gower was deeply shocked by the supercilious attitude to Orientals of the young Officers of the Seventy-fourth Regiment which was stationed in the Colony."

Lord Sheldon did not speak. Thinking that his expression was no less supercilious, she went on angrily:

" 'No wonder,' Lord Ronald wrote, 'we English are so disliked wherever we go. There is no-one more abhorrent to a foreigner than an English civilian, unless it be a Military Englishman!' "

Azalea made a gesture with both her hands.

"Does that mean nothing to you?" she asked. "No ... I am quite certain that if you had heard what Lord Ronald said, you would have swept it away as being much too humane to be tolerated by your stiff-necked superiority."

"Those are hard words!" Lord Sheldon said as Azalea paused for breath, "very hard words, and I could answer them with the same violence that you expended on me. Instead, I will quote you a Chinese proverb."

He spoke very quietly and because of it Azalea felt her anger subsiding a little.

"The proverb says: 'Sweet persuasion more effective than hard blows.' "

There was a smile on his lips as he finished speaking. Then to Azalea's astonishment he put out his arms and drew her close to him.

"I like your courage," he said. "Let me try and see if sweet persuasion will be effective."

Before she could answer him, before she could move, he put his fingers under her chin and turned her face up to his. Then, astonishingly, bewildering, his lips were on hers.

For a moment she was unable to move because she was so surprised. Then as she lifted her hands to press them against his chest and thrust him away from her, she felt his lips evoke a strange and utterly confounding sensation.

It was a feeling she had never known before in her whole life, and something warm and wonderful crept up through her whole body and into her throat and quivered on her lips beneath his.

It was an emotion such as she had never dreamt of or realised could be possible. A wonder which came from inside herself and was part of her whole being.

She could not understand it; she hardly believed it was possible. Only she was unable to move; unable to take her lips from his.

She felt his arms tighten a little round her, but still she could not thrust him away.

Vaguely at the back of her mind she thought that what was happening to her was part of the sunshine she had missed, the colour for which she had yearned, the music she had lost.

It was all there, in the glory and the wonder that was suddenly a rapture because a man was holding her mouth captive with his.

As he raised his head she looked up into his eyes and felt that he mesmerised her to the point when her brain no longer belonged to her but, like her lips, had become part of him.

Then with a little cry she turned from him to run blindly in a wild panic from the room. . . .

Chapter Two

"How could I have let him do it? How could I?" Azalea asked herself not once but a thousand times in the days that followed.

She hardly had a moment to think because there was so much packing to do before they finally left for Hong Kong, but at the back of her mind the question repeated itself over and over again, interspersed with the words:

"I hate him! I hate him!"

Lord Sheldon stood, she thought, for everything that she and her father had most disliked, the autocratic superior Englishman who despised those under his authority and who had no respect for any race except his own.

She knew that she should not have raged at him, but as she listened behind the curtains to what he was saying to his friend she had felt her anger rise like a flood-tide.

When he practically accused her of being a spy she could not control the words which burst from her lips.

In retrospect she thought it had probably been indiscreet of her to mention what Lord Ronald Gower had said.

She had found notes on his views in the file which the General had been given by the War Office on being told of his new appointment to Hong Kong.

Azalea knew she had no right to touch, let alone read, what were her Uncle's private papers, and the file was clearly marked "Hong Kong—Secret and Confidential."

But when on its arrival at Aldershot the General had left it casually on his desk, she had been unable to resist the temptation to glance inside.

Once she saw what it contained, her curiosity could not be assuaged until she had read everything in the file.

It was her job to pack up the General's belongings in the house they were occupying and to unpack them again when they arrived at Battlesdon House in Hampstead.

Azalea made it one of her jobs to dust and tidy the General's Study in what had been her grandfather's house, and every day she managed to read more and more of the memoranda, communications, and notes which were contained in the file on Hong Kong.

Most of the correspondence was from General Donovan, complaining about the Governor's new policies which, if he was to be believed, not only infuriated the Military authorities in the Colony, but also aroused alarm and anger amongst all the Europeans.

In fact, the only criticism of the Military came from Lord Ronald Gower.

His opinion had been brought to the notice of the War Office because, shocked by what he considered the boorish arrogance of the Officers of the Seventy-fourth Regiment, he had refused to tour Japan with a group of them who were going there on leave.

It was obvious to Azalea that her Uncle had every intention of maintaining the sterner attitude forcibly expressed by General Donovan.

"Donovan has the right idea!" he said to his wife during one meal at which Azalea was present. "I shall follow his methods in trying to keep the criminals in check with the threat of what will happen to them if they do not behave themselves. The Governor's 'mercy' programme has proved completely hopeless!"

"In what way?" Lady Osmund asked, but in a voice which told Azalea that she was not really interested.

"Robbery, murder, and arson are on the increase

since the Governor showed the populace that he was both weak and sentimental."

"What sort of crimes do they commit?" Azalea asked because she was so interested.

"Robbery is of course the most lucrative crime," her Uncle answered. "The Chinese, having inventive minds, use the storm-water drains to creep under the town and tunnel their way through into the vaults of banks, jewellery-stores, and what are known as the 'go-downs' of bigger merchants."

"Good Heavens!" Lady Osmund exclaimed. "They might tunnel their way into Flagstaff House!"

"You are quite safe, my dear," the General replied drily. "When the vaults of the Central Bank of Western India were broken into, the thieves got away with thousands of dollars in notes and eleven thousand pounds worth of gold ingots!"

"That was clever!" Azalea exclaimed before she could prevent herself.

Her Uncle gave her his usual contemptuous glance.

"Clever! That is hardly the word I would use to describe such criminals!" he said coldly. "Make no mistake, as soon as I arrive I shall advocate that public floggings and branding in the neck are reintroduced, and I shall make quite certain that the Governor's 'humane gaol' is very uncomfortable for these felons!"

"Do you really believe that such brutal methods will be an effective deterrent to crime?" Azalea enquired.

"I will make sure they are!" the General replied menacingly.

Lady Osmund did not appear to be interested. Her mind was too preoccupied with purchasing elegant dresses for the twins and being fitted for the evening-gowns she would wear at Government House, however much her husband might disapprove of the Governor.

The Government House in every British Colony was the focal point of social life, and Lady Osmund was, Azalea knew, quite certain that it was there that Violet and Daisy would meet the right sort of young men who would make them rich and commendable husbands.

She was, however, somewhat perturbed when she re-

turned to Battlesdon House one afternoon after taking
tea with the widow of the previous Colonel.

"Do you know what Lady Kennedy has told me,
Frederick?" she asked the General as soon as he returned.

"I have no idea," he replied.

"She tells me that there was an attempt made by the
Chinese to murder all the British by adding poison to
the bread they ate for breakfast! Is that true?"

The General hesitated a moment before he answered:

"It did happen—but a long time ago, in 1857 in
fact."

"But I understand that Lady Bowring, whose husband was then Governor of the Colony, became deliri-
ous and was forced to return to England, where she
died."

"I believe it is very debatable whether Lady
Bowring's death was the effect of poison or not," the
General replied. "In fact, the War Office reports affirm
that no deaths were directly attributable to the plot, although some people believed their health to be permanently undermined."

"But, Frederick, how can we go to a place with the
girls when we might be murdered with every mouthful
of food we eat?"

"I assure you, Emily, that the whole story has been
much exaggerated. What happened was that one bak-
ery, which was considered by European housewives to
make the best-quality bread, was found to have used
arsenic in considerable quantities both in their brown
and white loaves."

"It is terrible! Horrible to think about!" Lady Osmund exclaimed.

"I quite agree," the General said. "But in fact the
whole plot was instigated by the Mandarins of Canton
as part of their war of nerves, and the punishments inflicted on the perpetrators of the crime will, I am quite
certain, prove an effective deterrent for all time."

"I do not believe it!" Lady Osmund said. "And I assure you, Frederick, I am not going to put my chil-

dren's lives, and certainly not my own, in danger from those horrible, sinister Chinese!"

"I promise you, Emily, that your fears are exaggerated," the General answered.

"And what about the pirates?" Lady Osmund almost screamed. "Lady Kennedy tells me that they are a continual menace to shipping."

"That is correct," the General agreed.

"Then why isn't it stopped?"

"Because literally nothing is known about the bases of the pirates who prey on Hong Kong, nor of those who finance them, although we imagine the source is again Canton."

"Surely the Navy can do something?"

"We have gun-boats patrolling the harbour and the coastline, and we have set up a special Piracy Court and prohibited arms and munitions on Chinese junks."

"But it is ineffective!" Lady Osmund snapped.

"Piracy is less of a menace than robberies and burglaries by armed gangs."

"Armed?" Lady Osmund's exclamation was a shriek.

"It is undoubtedly the Governor's weak policy which encourages them!"

"Then you must challenge it!"

"That is exactly what I intend to do," the General replied grimly.

"Well, until you can do so I will not set foot on Hong Kong!"

It took great efforts on the part of the General to calm his wife down.

She reiterated over and over again that she was now afraid of going to Hong Kong!

Azalea felt with a sinking of her heart that, if she persisted in her attitude, not only would Lady Osmund and the twins not sail on the *Orissa* but she also would be left behind with them in England.

Fortunately, the importance of the General's position in Hong Kong overcame Lady Osmund's fears, and finally she agreed with a somewhat exaggerated show of reluctance to proceed with their plans.

Azalea, as it happened, had read about the arsenic plot and she could understand the horror the Europeans in Hong Kong had felt when one January morning at every breakfast table there arose the simultaneous cry of "Poison in the bread!"

There was a report of the occurrence in the General's file from which she had learnt that Doctors, themselves in pain, scurried from house to house and "emetics were in urgent request by every family."

But Azalea was not only concerned with European and Military difficulties in Hong Kong.

Ever since she was a child she had been fascinated by thoughts of the huge expanse of China, about which there was so much mystery and speculation.

She knew from what her mother had told her that the Chinese were great craftsmen and Azalea had learnt a little about the Confucian religion also from her.

Her grandfather had been a writer on philosophical subjects, which had inevitably led him to study the religions of the Orient.

His home was in the South of Russia where both the climate and the people were warm and friendly, but he had journeyed to India when he was a comparatively young man because he was interested in Hinduism and especially Yoga.

Once there, he had settled in the foothills of the Himalayas, where he had furthered both his studies and his writing.

It was on a visit to Lahore that Ivan Kharkov had met the daughter of a Russian Envoy to India.

He fell wildly, passionately in love, and after they were married and because they both adored India they decided to make it their home.

Azalea's mother, Feodorouna, who was their only child, was beautiful, graceful, and clever, as might have been expected with such unusually intelligent parents.

It was her beauty that had attracted Derek Osmund to her first, when he was spending his leave from the Army on a shooting expedition.

He used to say to Azalea:

"The moment I saw your mother I fell in love with her. She was the most beautiful and graceful creature I had ever seen in my whole life!"

Later Azalea learnt that he loved his wife's mind, her understanding and her sympathy, and even her strange emotional mysticism.

It was difficult for any European to understand the spiritual yearnings which motivated her, but she was extremely happy with Derek Osmund, and looking back Azalea could never remember hearing her father and mother quarrel.

'They both loved people, they both wanted to bring happiness to the world in which they lived,' she would think to herself when she was alone.

It was her mother who had taught her to see beauty not only in flowers, the birds, and the snow-capped mountain-peaks, but also in the colourful Bazaars, the moving kaleidoscope of people from all parts of India, and in the faith of those who bathed in the River Ganges.

'Everywhere Mama found beauty!' Azalea would often think.

Then she would try not to hate the coldness of the house where she lived with her Uncle and Aunt, the harshness of their voices, their expressions of anger, the manner in which they looked at her.

It was all so ugly, but she tried, although always in vain, to find, as she was certain her mother would have done, some beauty even in her Uncle's pomposity, or her Aunt's spiteful and unnecessary fault-finding.

Deep in her memory was the time when her mother had talked to her of the beauty of Jade which had been carved by the Chinese for thousands of years and of their paintings which were more artistic and more perceptive than those done by any other artists in the world.

She also told Azalea that the Chinese had an ingrained sense of honour and a scrupulous honesty, which was part of their character. Yet this seemed very much at variance with what her Uncle had to say about the Chinese in Hong Kong.

'It will be so wonderful to see for myself!' Azalea thought.

And yet the fear persisted in her mind that some catastrophe, some change of mind on her Aunt's part, or perhaps an order from the War Office, would at the very last moment prevent them from leaving.

The General sailed two days before them on a Troop Ship which carried reinforcements to the Colony.

Even then Azalea was half-afraid that illness or an accident would prevent them from reaching Tilbury, but her fears were groundless!

As they stepped out of the train to see the ship waiting for them at the Quay-side she felt her heart begin to beat with an excitement she had not known since she had left India.

Lady Osmund had been even more than usually disagreeable the last two days before they sailed, and it seemed to Azalea as if she could do nothing right.

Trunks that were packed had to be unpacked. Things which Lady Osmund had said were to be left behind were suddenly required to be taken with them, and the choice of clothes in which the twins were to travel was changed a dozen times.

Gowns arrived from the dress-maker at the very last moment; a sun-shade that was lost turned up in the kitchen, although no-one could explain how it could have got there.

When finally they drove away from Battlesdon House Azalea felt so tired that she was afraid she would fall asleep before they reached the railway station.

Her Aunt settled down to ask about dozens upon dozens of articles that had been packed but which she was certain had been forgotten.

Fortunately, Azalea had a good memory.

"In the round-topped trunk, Aunt Emily," she murmured. "In the square leather case." "In the tin trunk!" "In the valise!"

She had the answer to every question until finally her Aunt lapsed into silence.

The twins said nothing, although occasionally they giggled with each other.

They were pretty girls, almost identical in appearance, and with their fair hair, blue eyes, and pink-and-white skin were the perfect example of the ideal English debutante.

On the other hand, although mercifully not everyone noticed it, they were extremely stupid.

They seemed to be interested in nothing except each other. Even the young men whom Lady Osmund forced upon them, provided they were distinguished enough, evoked little more than monosyllabic replies and an endless succession of girlish giggles.

Azalea had heard one lady who was supposedly a friend of Lady Osmund's say scathingly:

"They have two bodies with only one mind between them, and a very tiny one at that!"

It was, Azalea had to admit, a more or less truthful comment, and yet she liked her cousins and they had never been anything but pleasant to her.

Dressed in new and very elegant travelling-gowns of rose-pink, their close-fitting jackets trimmed with fur, and their bonnets tied under their chins with satin ribbons, they looked very attractive.

In contrast, Azalea was well aware of the disparity in her own appearance.

There had been nothing suitable for her to travel in that had once belonged to the twins, and Lady Osmund, determined to economise where her niece was concerned, had presented her with a travelling-gown and jacket of her own which had proved an unfortunate purchase.

Dark chocolate-brown, it had been badly altered by the seamstress who came to the house, and although Azalea had tried with her own skilful fingers to make the gown fit better, nothing could change its unbecoming colour.

It made her skin look sallow and seemed to envelop her with a kind of inexpressible gloom.

"I hate it!" she told herself when she saw it lying on

her bed ready for her to put on for the journey. "It is ugly!"

She had at that moment a sudden longing for beautiful clothes; for the brilliant colours, the soft silks and transparent gauzes which her mother had worn.

They had made her skin glow like ivory and her hair hold purple and blue lights which at night seemed part of the moonlight.

But there was for Azalea only the brown dress, or else to board the ship in the March wind and rain wearing one of the thin, faded gowns which had been handed down to her by Violet or Daisy.

"No-one will look at me anyway," Azalea told herself sensibly, "and besides, I shall be very busy."

That was to understate what she knew lay ahead of her.

Lady Osmund made it quite clear that, if she was to enjoy the privilege of travelling with them, she would act as lady's-maid to all three.

"I would have taken a cabin on the Second-Class deck for you," she said to Azalea, "but that might make it difficult for you to spend your time with us. Therefore you are very fortunate, and you should be very grateful for being allowed to travel First Class."

"Thank you, Aunt Emily," Azalea said, knowing that the reply was expected of her.

She was not, however, inclined to be so grateful when she saw her cabin.

Lady Osmund and the twins had outside cabins on the First-Class deck. They were spacious and light and were furnished in a manner which justified the P.&O. eulogising about them.

Azalea's cabin had no port-hole and was so small as to have been, she was quite certain, intended only for a servant, or perhaps when the ship was not full, for a store-room.

But, she told herself quietly, what did it matter as long as the ugly square-prowed *Orissa*, with its two slightly leaning funnels which gave it a vacuous look, would carry her to Hong Kong.

She was well aware that the Shipping Lines were intensely proud of their ships and advertised them extravagantly.

Her Uncle had left a brochure lying on his desk, and reading it Azalea had learnt that the engines were "so smooth it was difficult to believe the ship was moving at all."

There was an organ, a picture-gallery, and a Library which contained over three hundred books!

This, Azalea told herself, was the first place she would visit as soon as she had an opportunity.

Lady Osmund swept up the gangway of the *Orissa* rather as if she herself were a ship in full sail.

She told the Purser condescendingly that she was prepared to look at the State-Rooms that had been allotted to her and hoped that they would be to her satisfaction.

She then asked if Lord Sheldon was on board, and was annoyed to find that he had not yet arrived.

"The Commander-in-Chief himself has requested His Lordship to look after us," she told the Purser. "Kindly ask His Lordship to notify me as soon as he comes aboard."

"I'll do that, M'Lady," the Purser replied.

He went on to ask about Lady Osmund's other requirements in such a mollifying and pleasant manner that Her Ladyship finally condescended to accept the State-Rooms without comment.

As soon as the luggage was brought aboard, knowing what was expected of her, Azalea took off her jacket and bonnet and started to unpack.

She arranged her Aunt's clothes first, hanging them neatly in the fitted wardrobe and placing her tortoise-shell toilet set with its golden initials on the built-in dressing-table.

This took her some time and after she had called for a steward to remove the empty trunks she began to unpack for the twins.

They had gone on deck to see the ship sail, and soon there were the blowing of whistles, the clanging of gongs, and the music of the Band vibrating above the "chug" of the engines as the ship began to proceed slowly from the Quay and out into the river.

Azalea would have liked to go on deck too, but she told herself it would undoubtedly annoy her Aunt and it would be best for her first to finish hanging up the twins' evening-gowns.

"I shall have a chance to explore the ship later," Azalea told herself, and wondered what books would be available in the Library.

She had scoured the General's study at Battlesdon House before she left and had discovered only one small volume on Chinese art written some years earlier.

Greatly daring, she had packed it in her own trunk so that she would be able to read it while they were at sea.

On the way back from India she had had a great deal of time on her hands during the twenty-four-day journey.

But she then had nothing else to do but feel miserable and try to make herself realise that her father was dead, and that her home in the future must be with her Uncle, of whom she was afraid.

Now she was quite certain that with three of them to look after she would be kept busy.

At the same time, she was going back to the sunshine, to the East, which for her would always be home, and she knew there was so much for her to learn if she was to understand and appreciate Hong Kong.

It was to be expected that Azalea should be very quick at learning languages.

She had spoken Russian with her mother and as a baby she had been sung to sleep with Russian lullabies. She could both read and speak French. She had conversed with the Indian servants in Urdu since she could first talk.

Her father had been criticised in the Regiment because he could speak to his Sepoys and the coolies in their own language.

"Let them learn English!" his fellow-Officers had said, but Derek Osmund had paid no attention.

Besides this, which was unusual in an Englishmen, he positively enjoyed speaking languages other than his own.

"I must learn Chinese," Azalea told herself.

But she was not quite certain how to go about it and was sure that if her Aunt heard of her intention she would be forbidden to do anything of the sort.

When Lady Osmund and the twins came to the cabin after Azalea had nearly finished emptying the very last trunk, they were obviously all in good humour.

"It is a lovely ship, Azalea!" Violet exclaimed. "And there are lots of exciting people on board."

"I would not go so far as to say that," Lady Osmund said reprovingly, "but Lord Sheldon is a passenger and you will both make yourselves very pleasant to him."

The twins giggled and Azalea turned her head aside in case her Aunt should notice the colour rising in her cheeks.

She had not faced asking herself how she would feel when she had to meet Lord Sheldon again.

How could he have kissed her? And how, while he did so, had she stayed in his arms instead of fighting violently against him or screaming for help?

He must have hypnotised her, she thought. Then she remembered that strange, sweet, unaccountable sensation that his kiss had evoked.

She had only to think of it to remember the warm and wonderful feeling that had crept through her whole body until it seemed to end in her lips.

"It was an illusion . . . part of my imagination!" she said severely.

Yet she knew that what she had felt had been an inexpressible rapture, and however severe she was with herself, however much she tried to deny it, she longed to feel the marvel of it again.

'He is despicable, conceited, autocratic, and altogether abominable!' she reiterated in her mind.

Yet whatever his character, he had aroused a response in her that she could never forget.

She tried to remember if in all her reading she had ever come across a description of anything so complex.

How could one hate and despise a man, and yet be aroused by him in a manner that was so perfect that there was something spiritual as well as physical in its very wonder?

"I am just ignorant and confused," Azalea told herself, and yet she was intelligent enough to know that that was not the proper answer.

"Dinner will be at seven o'clock," Lady Osmund announced.

The sharpness of her tone made Azalea jump because her thoughts had been far away.

"Am ... am I to ... dine with you, Aunt Emily?" she asked humbly.

"I suppose so," Lady Osmund replied grudgingly, "but I do not expect you to push yourself forward! Not that I imagine anyone will take much notice of you."

She paused and her eyes flickered over her niece unpleasantly.

"After all, we cannot pretend you are not a relation, even though it is nothing of which we can be proud!" she said spitefully. "But poor relations are expected to be humble and subservient; so you will make no effort to join in the conversation and you will certainly not speak unless you are spoken to."

"I understand, Aunt Emily."

Feeling she must not show that she minded such admonition, Azalea went quietly from the cabin to start unpacking for herself.

She had with her a much more varied wardrobe than she had ever owned before, since Violet and Daisy had been provided with what was a complete new trousseau.

Therefore, contrary to what had happened in the past, the clothes Azalea had received from them were in good condition and comparatively new and fashionable.

They were, however, too fancy and too be-frilled to be becoming to her slender figure. Although she contrived to remove some of the ruchings, fringes, braiding, and bows, which she thought made them look like Christmas-trees, there was nothing she could do about the pale colours which somehow looked wrong against the darkness of her hair.

"But, as Aunt Emily said," Azalea told herself, "no-one is going to look at me!"

However, she put on a gown which she felt was the most attractive of all the gowns she now owned, remembering as she did so that her mother had once said that first impressions were important.

But there was another thought at the back of her mind which she hardly dared admit to herself.

Lord Sheldon, before he had kissed her in that outrageous fashion, had asked her what was her position in the house.

He had thought her too cultured for a house-maid, but he had never for one moment thought she might in fact be a lady.

Very well, there was a surprise in store for him!

He would find that she was not only a lady, but the General's niece as well!

That was not a circumstance which Azalea personally thought was much of a recommendation, but Lord Sheldon, with his conventional, hide-bound ideas, would undoubtedly be impressed by Uncle Frederick as a distinguished soldier.

Azalea therefore took a little more trouble than usual in arranging her dark hair.

Usually she coiled it into a thick chignon and pinned it at the back of her small head. Tonight she made it look a little more fashionable, but was aware that to arrange it in curls such as her cousins wore would cause her Aunt to make some very sarcastic comments.

When she was ready she glanced at herself in the mirror and thought with a little smile that, while she might not look very attractive, she certainly did not have the appearance of a cultured house-maid or some-one who was giving a hand to help out an overburdened staff.

She wondered if there would be a look of surprise in Lord Sheldon's eyes.

It was difficult to forget how penetratingly he had looked at her when he had questioned her as to why she was eavesdropping on the conversation he had had with his friend.

"How dare he be suspicious of me!" Azalea exclaimed aloud.

She tried to tell herself that she hated him violently to the point where she would be glad to learn he was injured or even swept overboard to drown.

Then she could only remember the strange, demanding warmth of his lips, and hastily turned towards the door.

There was her Aunt's gown to fasten, the twins to be buttoned into their dresses, and ribbons to be threaded through their hair before the party was ready to descend to the Dining-Saloon.

Lady Osmund went ahead, her train, be-frilled and rouched, rustling out behind her like the waves in the wake of a ship.

The twins followed, walking hand in hand as they usually did and giggling a little at nothing in particular. Azalea brought up the rear.

The First-Class Dining-Saloon was very impressive. The passengers sat in arm-chairs at the various tables which were covered with heavy white linen cloths, and there seemed to be a whole army of stewards in white coats in attendance.

There were pot-plants in the corners of the Saloon and at the Captain's table, where naturally Lady Osmund and her party were to sit, and because it was the first night at sea, there was a table-decoration of flowers and green leaves.

Lady Osmund sat at the Captain's right, although that night he was not present because, as was traditional, he was on the bridge, navigating the ship safely out to sea.

The twins sat next to their mother and Azalea next to the twins. That left a place on her right, which when they entered the Dining-Saloon was vacant.

There were about ten other places at the Captain's table, most of them occupied by people to whom Lady

Osmund had either already been introduced or had known before she came aboard.

The gentlemen stood up while she seated herself and the ladies bowed and smiled.

A General was always of importance, especially one who had been knighted, and Hong Kong was an important harbour from the point of view of the British Empire.

Those who smiled ingratiatingly at Lady Osmund were wondering how useful it would be in the future to know the G.O.C. commanding a Port-of-Call, and Hong Kong was undoubtedly a stepping stone to a most important position.

A steward hurried forward with the menus, and without consulting either her daughters or Azalea, Lady Osmund ordered what they would eat. While she herself drank wine, the twins and Azalea were given water.

The first course was just being served when Azalea was aware that a man had joined the party at their table and was seating himself beside her.

She glanced up and then felt, with a sudden shock, her heart begin to beat unaccountably within her breast.

It was Lord Sheldon who sat beside her, and as she looked away from him hastily she felt that he must have seen the blush that rose almost painfully in her cheeks.

But if she was embarrassed Lord Sheldon was entirely at his ease.

"Good-evening, Miss Osmund!" he said. "I hope you are looking forward to the journey?"

Then as he asked the question the steward presented him with the menu and he scanned it while he still seemed to be waiting for Azalea's reply.

For a moment it was impossible to speak. Lord Sheldon gave his order, then turned his attention to the wine-waiter who handed him a leather-bound wine-list. Finally he looked at Azalea.

"Are you a good sailor?" he asked.

"I think so," Azalea managed to answer in what she

hoped was a cool, calm voice, but which sounded a little breathless. "I have only been to sea once before."

"And when was that?"

They might, Azalea thought, have been meeting for the first time at a Vicarage tea-party; but because the manner in which her heart was behaving made it difficult to reply, it required a superhuman effort for her to manage to say:

"Two years ago . . . when I came from India."

She thought Lord Sheldon looked surprised as he asked:

"From India? So you know that country?"

"It is my home."

Azalea could not help speaking a little defiantly.

"Why?"

It was only one word and yet she knew that he was interested.

"My parents lived there—my father was in the same Regiment as my Uncle."

She wondered as she spoke if she was saying too much. Then she told herself that her Uncle could not expect her to conceal the fact that her father had served in what was to all intents and purposes the family Regiment, as his father and grandfather had done before him.

Besides, she told herself, there was nothing to hide except the manner in which he had met his death.

She knew she should have anticipated that sometime these questions would be asked, but she had lived such an isolated existence since she had gone to live with her Uncle and Aunt.

She had been to no parties or Receptions of any sort, and it had never occurred to her that she might one day have a conversation such as this, and with, of all people, Lord Sheldon!

"So at one time your father was stationed at Lahore?"

"Yes."

Azalea made up her mind that the only way to protect herself would be to reply to his questions in monosyllables.

He might think her dull and nit-witted, but at least he would not think she was trying to grab or claw at him, nor would he dare to describe her as a "man-eating tiger-cub."

The steward poured out His Lordship's wine and he tasted it.

"I always think Lahore is one of the most beautiful cities in India," he said reflectively. "The city of roses."

Azalea could not answer as the memory of the roses in Lahore brought her a sudden pain and a sense of home-sickness that was a physical agony.

She could see her mother coming in from the garden carrying a whole armful of them. She could smell the fragrance now and knew that their beauty was there, stored in her memory, more vivid and more real than anything that had happened to her since she had left India behind.

"Where else in India have you been?" Lord Sheldon asked.

"Many places," Azalea answered, hoping he would think her stupid.

"I am sure that among them you have seen your namesake in the foothills of the Himalayas. I cannot believe that anything could be more beautiful than when the azaleas are in bloom and the snow still lies on the mountain-peaks."

He spoke quietly but again his words evoked a memory that was hard to bear.

If only he knew, Azalea thought wildly, how she had lain awake night after night thinking of the azaleas gold and red, crimson, pink and white, and wishing that once again she could be amongst them.

She could remember saying to her mother:

"Why did you call me Azalea, Mama?"

Her mother had laughed.

"What could be a more perfect name? Your grand-father had said that all his granddaughters were to be given the names of flowers, and when you were born, my dearest, I could look from my window onto a rain-bow that had fallen from the sky.

" 'What are you going to call her?' your father asked me.

"I smiled up at him from the bed where I was holding you in my arms."

" 'Have we any choice?' I questioned.

"He looked out the window and laughed.

" 'But of course—she must be called Azalea! And may she be as beautiful and as fragrant as the flower itself—or as her mother!' "

"You have not answered my question," Lord Sheldon prompted her.

"Yes . . . I have seen the azaleas in the spring," she answered, and had no idea there was a throb in her voice that had not been there before.

A man seated on the other side of Lord Sheldon engaged him in conversation, and Azalea felt she had time to get her breath and hope the agitation within her breast would gradually fade away.

How could she have imagined that of all people she would sit next to the man who had kissed her in her Uncle's Study and had first thought her to be a spy and then a servant?

She glanced down the table at her Aunt and realised that she was annoyed that Lord Sheldon should be beside her.

She beckoned with her finger and obediently Azalea rose and went to her side.

"You will change places with Violet," she said sharply. "There is no reason for the girls always to sit together in this childish manner."

It was an excuse, Azalea knew well, to move her from Lord Sheldon's proximity, and while she told herself it would save her from further embarrassment, she could not help regretting being unable to continue their conversation about India.

He would not have appreciated the country anyway, she told herself. He would have been too busy bullying his Indian servants or drilling the soldiers unmercifully in the heat.

But there had been something in his voice when he spoke of the azaleas that told her, to her surprise, that he appreciated their beauty, they had meant something to him.

Could anyone, Azalea asked herself, see such beauty and not long for it again? Even anyone as stiff-necked and unimaginative as Lord Sheldon must be?

She moved Violet into her place and sat down between the two girls.

Although Lord Sheldon was talking to the man on his other side she had a feeling, although she could not substantiate it, that he was aware of what had happened and that it was her Aunt who had effected the change.

As Azalea thought that nothing would appear more dull and in fact ruder than that three girls should sit in a row and say nothing to each other, she started to talk to Daisy.

"You must learn to talk and listen, Azalea," her mother had said to her when first she had been allowed to have luncheon and dinner in the Dining-Room. "There is nothing more boring than a woman, however pretty she is, who has nothing to say and does not give the right sort of sympathetic attention when people talk to her."

"And what is the right sort?" Azalea had asked.

She had not been very old at the time.

"It is right to take a sincere interest in other people; their troubles, their difficulties, their joys, and their sorrows," her mother replied. "When you once begin to think of them as having the same feelings as yourself, you will find yourself automatically making friends. Friendship, Azalea, is when you share part of yourself with another person."

Azalea had never forgotten her mother's words, and although sometimes she found it hard to think of the more austere Officers and their chattering, gossip-loving wives as like herself, she did try to give them her sympathy and listen to what they had to say.

She remembered her father once speaking angrily and rather scathingly about the wife of an Officer who was making trouble for the other wives.

"She is a spiteful woman and if she has a heart no-one has yet found it!"

"I am sorry for her," Azalea's mother had said softly.

"Sorry for her?" Derek Osmund exclaimed in surprise. "But why?"

"Because she must be so unhappy," his wife replied. "If she has nothing to give the world except criticism and malice, think what she must be like inside and what she has to suffer from herself when she is alone."

Azalea remembered that her father, after looking at her mother incredulously for a moment, had then put his arms round her.

"You would find excuses for the very devil himself, my darling!"

"And why not?" Mrs. Osmund asked. "After all, he has to spend the whole of his existence in hell!"

Azalea's father had laughed but she had often remembered her mother's words.

Perhaps, she sometimes told herself, her Aunt, because she was so bitter, cruel, and unkind, was in fact suffering, although it was hard to believe that she did not enjoy making people, and herself in particular, unhappy.

Perhaps when the General was alone he was no longer pompous and overwhelmingly superior, but afraid because he was growing old that he might be passed over for a younger man.

'How am I to know,' Azalea thought, 'what such people think and feel unless I can talk to them?'

She wondered if she would ever be able to talk intimately to her Aunt or her Uncle. It was very unlikely!

The dinner, which consisted of a large number of courses, none of which had been outstandingly delectable, came to an end and Lady Osmund rose from the table.

As she passed Lord Sheldon she paused and he got to his feet.

"I hope you will join us in the lounge for coffee," she said graciously.

"You must forgive me, Ma'am," he replied, "but I have some very important work to do."

"In that case, I will say good-night."

"Good-night, Lady Osmund."

He bowed as she moved away from the table.

The twins passed him, giggling again with each other, and then his eyes rested on Azalea.

She told herself she would not look at him, but somehow, as if he compelled her to do so, as she reached him she raised her eyes involuntarily to his.

The expression on his face made her feel shy and embarrassed.

"Good-night, Miss Azalea," he said very quietly.

She wanted to answer him but somehow the words would not come.

Quickly, with the grace of a frightened fawn, she turned and hurried after the twins.

She wanted to look back but she did not dare.

Only as she reached the top of the stairway which led from the Dining-Saloon did she feel the thumping of her heart begin to subside and know that once again she could speak normally.

Chapter Three

Lord Sheldon walked unsteadily to the Captain's table in the Dining-Saloon to find that he was the only passenger there.

There were half a dozen men at other tables in the room, somewhat green about the gills and turning away most of the dishes the stewards offered to them, but the large Saloon was otherwise empty.

It was not surprising that there was such a sparse attendance, seeing that the sea had been unprecedentedly rough since they had left England.

"There's not much more the *Orissa* can do, M'Lord, except stand on her head!" said the steward who had called Lord Sheldon that morning.

Even as he spoke he had been flung across the cabin and only managed to retain his balance by holding on to the bed.

"I imagine most of the passengers are not enjoying the voyage," Lord Sheldon remarked.

"Nearly everyone of them's prostrate, M'Lord," the steward replied, "and as Your Lordship can imagine, we're run off our feet."

Lord Sheldon certainly gave little trouble.

He was a good sailor and enjoyed the sea. When he had taken some exercise, being the only person in sight on the wave-washed deck, the storm gave him a good excuse to get on with his writing.

It might be uncomfortable to write at strange angles and to have to fasten his ink-pot down securely, but it

was to his mind far more agreeable than having to
chatter to the many woman on board.

They invariably pursued him relentlessly in what
they fondly imagined was an unobtrusive manner but
which he found both embarrassing and a bore.

There had been no sign of Lady Osmund, Lord
Sheldon thought with satisfaction as he ordered quite a
large luncheon, since the first night at sea.

She was the type of Army wife whom he disliked,
and he could not help remembering how George
Widcombe had disparaged her and that her aspirations
as far as he was concerned were extremely obvious.

He was sorry for any man who was finally caught
for either of the Osmund twins in the matrimonial net.

Apart from the fact that the girls had little brain and
even less personality, whoever they married would always be overpowered both by Lady Osmund and the
General.

It was strange, Lord Sheldon thought to himself,
that two such unprepossessing people, although he did
not question the General's Military ability, should have
Azalea as a niece.

He had not seen her again since the first dinner
aboard, but he supposed that she, like every other
woman on the *Orissa,* had succumbed to the tempest.

As the steward offered Lord Sheldon the first course
he had ordered, having difficulty keeping his balance as
he did so, His Lordship remarked:

"I appear to be alone in my glory."

"We are certainly not overworked at the Captain's
table, M'Lord," the steward replied. "The Captain has
been on the bridge since we left harbour and has not
been down for a single meal. You and Miss Osmund
are the only passengers we have the pleasure of serving."

"Miss Osmund?" Lord Sheldon questioned.

"Yes, M'Lord, but she comes early for luncheon and
dinner. Not a very social-minded young lady, if I may
say so."

Lord Sheldon did not reply; he was thinking of what
the steward had said.

Now he remembered that he had imagined he caught a glimpse of Azalea only the day before. Then he had told himself he must be mistaken, for he had seen a figure that he thought resembled her on the Second-Class deck.

He wondered why she should be visiting someone who was not travelling in the same class as she was herself.

Lord Sheldon had seen the passenger-list when he came aboard. It was his invariable habit to have the list sent to him by the Shipping Company with his ticket, so that he could know who were to be his fellow-travellers on long and often tedious voyages.

It was when he read the passenger-list that he had realised the identity of Azalea.

The Commander-in-Chief had merely asked him to look after Lady Osmund and her twin daughters.

When he had seen their three names tabulated and after them "Miss Azalea Osmund," he had known that his behaviour in the Study at Battlesdon House had been somewhat reprehensible.

And yet how, he asked himself, could Lady Osmund and the General have produced a daughter who was so unlike her sisters?

The Purser had enlightened him as soon as he came aboard.

"Lady Osmund was asking for you, M'Lord. She would be grateful if you would kindly notify her of your arrival."

The Purser had pointed to the plan of the ship in front of him.

"Lady Osmund is in Cabin B," he said, "Miss Violet and Miss Daisy Osmund are in Cabin C, and Miss Azalea is on the other side of the passage in Cabin J."

Lord Sheldon had looked at the position of the cabins as they were pointed out to him, and the Purser, as if he guessed at his unspoken comment, remarked:

"Miss Azalea Osmund is only a niece, M'Lord."

She might be "only a niece," as the Purser had said somewhat disparagingly, Lord Sheldon thought, but that did not really explain why she had not attended

the farewell party the General had given at Battlesdon
House or why she had been wearing a servant's apron.

It was a mystery and Lord Sheldon enjoyed mys-
teries.

He had, in fact, while he was in India, been very
much more than a successful soldier.

Those who knew that country, and the difficulties
and perils encountered there by the British troops,
were aware that there was within the Indian Administration an amazing system of espionage that extended
from the Northern Passes to the Southernmost tip of
the country.

All sorts of conditions of different peoples passed information in various ways to the Government, and
their identity was never revealed beyond the number
by which they were known to each other.

Lord Sheldon had been "C-27" and, when he com-
municated with a certain horse-dealer in the Punjab
who was known as "M-4," the information he obtained
from him might go to a Banker in Peshawar who was
"R-19," or a Moslem employed as an agent in a
Rajput state who was "N-46."

Known as "The Great Game," it was one of the
most amazing, intricate, and exciting phenomona of
English rule, and Lord Sheldon had worked his way to
a position of importance.

He had been taught by his instructors that the
slightest mistake, the faintest carelessness, could cause
loss of life which might well be his own.

He was therefore naturally alert and also continually
suspicious of anything out of the ordinary. Azalea, innocent though she might appear, had eavesdropped in
a manner which made him unlikely to dismiss it as
negligible.

He was also aware of the source from which her information had come regarding Lord Ronald Gower.

He had himself read the Hong Kong file after re-
ceiving his instructions from the Earl of Kimberly,
Secretary of State for the Colonies, and having had a
confidential interview with the Chief of Staff at the War
Office.

He had never thought of Sir Frederick Osmund as a talkative man, nor did he seem the type who would discuss official secrets with a girl, even if she was his niece.

It was therefore obvious to Lord Sheldon that, since Azalea had obviously read the Hong Kong file, she had done so without her Uncle's knowledge.

"But why?" he asked himself. "And for what purpose?"

Why, moreover, was her appearance so very un-English, especially in the company of her pink-and-white cousins?

He had in fact after their encounter at the dinner-table looked forward to probing further into Miss Azalea Osmund's strange behaviour.

There was, he told himself, plenty of time, and although he expected her not to appear until the ship reached the Mediterranean, he had every intention of pursuing his enquiries further before they reached Hong Kong.

Now, after what the steward had said, Lord Sheldon wondered if he had in fact been somewhat complacent over what was undoubtedly a mystery involving Military secrets.

Recalling what he had read in the confidential file on Hong Kong, he did not think there was anything particularly important about the long correspondence from General Donovan, the reports on the Military position, the Governor's unpopularity, and the manner in which he had changed the laws.

At the same time, a confidential report was not for outside eyes, and certainly it contained some information which could be utilised by enemy agents.

Lord Sheldon was quite determined to get to the bottom of the problem, but it was not his way when dealing with such affairs to rush in bald-headed without having all the facts he required at his finger-tips.

Moreover, he could not believe that Azalea, if she was a spy, was a very effective one.

He had heard the noise she had made inadvertently

with her feet on the floor, which was something no-one efficient in the art of espionage would have done.

There was also, he thought, evidence of inexperience both in her fear when she had come from behind the curtains to find him still in the Study and her undoubted panic when she had run away from him after he had kissed her.

Lord Sheldon was not prepared to explain to himself why he had done so. It had been an impulse which on reflection he did not regret.

When he finished luncheon he decided to go down to the Third-Class deck to enquire after the wife of a Company Sergeant Major who was journeying to Hong Kong to be with her husband, who had preceded her the week before.

The Sergeant Major had served with Lord Sheldon in India, and when it had been impossible for his wife to sail with him on the Troop Ship because she had only just produced a baby, he had called to see His Lordship.

"How did you know I was going to Hong Kong?" Lord Sheldon enquired when the Company Sergeant Major had arrived from Aldershot at his flat in St. James.

"It was in the newspapers, M'Lord, and as soon as I read it, I realised that you and the wife would be on the same ship. I worry about her travelling alone with the children. She's not one for the sea."

Lord Sheldon wondered with an inward smile how many soldiers' wives were, but he replied:

"I will certainly keep an eye on your wife, Sergeant Major, and I only hope the weather is not too rough."

"That's what I'm hoping too, M'Lord. I was never much of a sailor me self."

They talked of old times and then the Sergeant Major said:

"We miss you, M'Lord. Those of us who was with you in India wish we was back there, even if it was stinkin' 'ot at times!"

"I feel the same," Lord Sheldon smiled.

"Do you miss the Regiment, M'Lord? It don't seem right to be seeing you out of uniform."

"I miss it more than I can say," Lord Sheldon replied with a note of sincerity in his voice, "and I miss India. I am afraid you will find Hong Kong rather restricting. It is a very small Colony."

"That's just what I was thinking meself, M'Lord," the Sergeant Major said. "But I'm hopin' it won't be for long, and we'll have some Indian troops with us, which'll make it seem more like 'ome."

"It will indeed," Lord Sheldon agreed.

He had known that a number of Indian troops were being sent to Hong Kong to reinforce the Garrison, and that Officers and N.C.O.'s who had previously served in India were being drafted there to command them.

As the Sergeant Major had expected, his wife had succumbed immediately to the roughness of the sea, and although Lord Sheldon had sent her various comforts, the Stewardess who looked after her had reported that she was far from well.

Now descending to the Third-Class deck with some difficulty owing to the pitching and tossing of the vessel, Lord Sheldon moved along the narrow passageway to the cabin occupied by Mrs. Favel and her children.

The Third-Class arrangements in the *Orissa* were better than in many of the ships on which Lord Sheldon had sailed, but the passengers were nevertheless uncomfortably crowded.

Low down in the ship the smell of oil, bilge, and the lack of fresh air was very obvious, and only Lord Sheldon's sense of duty made him enquire personally every day about Mrs. Favel from the Stewardness who attended her.

He found her now without much difficulty, a middle-aged woman, looking tired and somewhat harassed as she came out of the cabin, carrying in her hands a bowl from which Lord Sheldon averted his eyes.

"I won't be a moment, M'Lord," the Stewardess said as she saw him and disappeared through a door where he could hear rushing water as she sluiced the bowl clean.

She came back wiping her hands and smiling.

Women of all ages and all classes invariably smiled at Lord Sheldon. There was something not only handsome but also attractive about him which they found irresistible.

"How is our patient?" Lord Sheldon asked.

"A bit more perky today, M'Lord, and very grateful for the bottle of brandy you sent her."

"I hope it helped her sea-sickness."

"I've always found there's nothing like brandy," the Stewardess said, "but unfortunately, M'Lord, few people on this deck can afford it."

"Let me know when Mrs. Favel wants another bottle," Lord Sheldon said, "and tell her I have enquired after her."

"She'll be very honoured, M'Lord. She has told me how much her husband admires Your Lordship."

"Thank you," Lord Sheldon said. "Is there anything else you want?"

"Nothing, thank you, M'Lord. I am just praying it won't be long before we reach a bit of calmer weather. I've never known it as bad as this."

"I suspect that is what you say every time there is a storm," Lord Sheldon remarked.

The Stewardess laughed.

"I expect you're right, M'Lord. One forgets until the next time, thank goodness!"

She spoke so fervently that Lord Sheldon also laughed and turned to go back the way he had come. Then he paused.

"By the way, how are the children?"

As he spoke he noticed for the first time how empty the passages were.

On other visits he had found children running about, quarrelling with each other and shrieking at the tops of their voices with a shrillness that echoed above the noise of the engines and the splash of the waves.

"The baby's all right, M'Lord," the Stewardess answered, "and the other two are with the kind lady that has been keeping them amused for the last two days. She seems like an angel of light to us, I can tell you!"

"What kind lady?" Lord Sheldon asked.

"I don't know her name," the Stewardess replied, "but she's a First-Class passenger who offered to take the children off our hands for several hours a day. It's been a blessing. Little devils they've been, every one of them, while their parents were ill, making a mess everywhere, and so noisy one could hardly hear oneself think!"

"Where are they now?" Lord Sheldon asked with some curiosity.

"In the Second-Class Writing-Room," the Stewardess replied. "That's dead against regulations, M'Lord, but who'd want to write a letter in this weather?"

"Who indeed?" Lord Sheldon answered.

There was a scream of "Stewardess!" from one of the cabins and the Stewardess hurried towards the door.

"Here we go again!" she ejaculated, and with the basin in her hand she disappeared through an adjacent door.

Climbing back to the Second-Class deck, Lord Sheldon hesitated for a moment as if he wondered which way he should go. Then he moved towards where he knew the Writing-Room would be situated.

The Second-Class deck had fewer recreational facilities than the First-Class.

In the Second-Class Saloon the passengers sat at long communal tables with their chairs "cheek-by-jowl" to avoid using too much room.

The Saloon was pleasantly furnished, but with very little space between the sofas and chairs, and beyond it was a small Writing-Room which was seldom used except by those who wanted to write or play cards without being interrupted by the chatter of voices.

Lord Sheldon crossed the Saloon towards it, and as his hand went out towards the door he heard a voice saying with pretence gruffness:

"Who's been sleeping in my bed?"

The voice rose a little.

"And the Mother Bear said: 'Who's been sleeping in my bed?'"

There was a pause and then a very high voice went on:

"And the Baby Bear said: 'Who's been sleeping in my bed—and there she is!'"

There were shrieks of childish delight before the narrator finished:

"Then Goldilocks jumped up and ran down the stairs and back to the safety of her mother's arms as quickly as she could!"

There was a babble of excitement and very gently Lord Sheldon opened the door a crack so that he could look into the room.

Seated on the floor with a small Chinese child in her arms was Azalea. The child was asleep, his dark eye-lashes like half-moons on his little round face.

Seated all round her, cross-legged or half-lying, were fifteen or sixteen other children.

They all seemed to be very young and many of them were poorly dressed, but they were all looking happy and even though she had finished the story they made no effort to move.

"What would you like to do now?" Lord Sheldon heard Azalea ask in her soft voice.

"Sing the clap-hands song!" a small boy suggested.

"Very well," Azalea said. "We will sing the song where you clap your hands, but as Jam Kin is asleep I cannot show you where to clap, so I will raise one hand . . . do you understand?"

There was a murmur of "yes" and a nodding of small heads.

"Very well," Azalea said, "when I raise my hand—clap!"

Lord Sheldon smiled as he saw how ready the children were to do what she suggested.

Very quietly he closed the door as he had opened it.

The last thing he wanted to do was disturb either Azalea or the children, but as he turned away he stopped suddenly.

Azalea had started to sing and her voice sounded

gay. He was sure it was a folk-song, but—she was singing in Russian!

It had been entirely Azalea's idea that she should keep the children occupied.

She had expected, once the ship had started to roll, that she would be constantly in attendance upon her Aunt, but the P.&O. Doctor was used to voyages which invariably started with a rough and tumble in the Bay of Biscay.

As soon as Lady Osmund began to complain querulously and incessantly about how ill she felt he provided her with what he called his "Soothing Syrup," two teaspoonsful of which kept her asleep for most of the day.

The twins, after being extremely sea-sick were quite prepared to lie in their bunks talking to each other and make no effort to get up.

They did not want Azalea, and apart from the fact that she washed and ironed their night-gowns, there was very little she need do for them.

When she learnt, therefore, from the Stewardess of the enormous amount of work caused by the other sea-sick passengers, she offered to help.

"We can't allow you to do that, Miss," the Stewardesses said. "You're First Class and the Purser would have a fit if he thought we were putting on you."

"You would not be doing that," Azalea assured them, "I work very hard when I am at home."

"You don't have to pay for it," the Stewardess retorted, "and being First Class on the *Orissa* entitles you to every comfort."

"There must be something I can do," Azalea insisted.

The Stewardess had hesitated.

"You have thought of something?"

"I don't think as I ought to mention it, Miss. I'll get into trouble—I know I will!"

"I promise you that will not happen," Azalea said, "but do let me help you."

"Well, it's just that there's a Chinese lady in the Second Class. She's ever so nice, Miss, much nicer than I ever thought the Chinese would be, but she's really sick and she's got a little boy."

"I will help you look after him," Azalea said before the Stewardess could say any more.

"If she could just get a quiet sleep in the afternoons she'd be all right," the Stewardess said. "But you know what a child of a year old is like! Crawling about the cabin, wanting a drink when I've just settled her down, asking for this and asking for that."

"Is she travelling alone?" Azalea asked.

"No, she's got her husband with her, but he's very grand! Chinese men! They don't wait on their wives, they expect to be waited upon!"

"So I have always heard," Azalea said with a smile. "Let me come and see this lady."

"I don't know that you should," the Stewardess protested.

But finally Azalea overruled all the difficulties and found herself meeting Mrs. Chang, who, to her surprise, was younger than Azalea was herself.

Although she was ill, Mrs. Chang was to Azalea's eyes one of the loveliest people she had ever seen.

With her hair so black that it was almost blue, drawn back from her perfect oval forehead, crow's-feather eye-brows, slanting eyes, and cupid's-bow mouth, she had an exotic odalisque beauty.

Jam Kin was the most adorable child imaginable.

In his long trousers and little satin coat that buttoned at the neck, he seemed to Azalea like a toy, and even when he sat on her knee she could hardly believe he was real.

Mrs. Chang spoke quite good English, and when Azalea sat on the floor of her cabin and played with Jam Kin she soon learnt that Mr. Chang was much older than his wife and a very important merchant in Hong Kong.

She also guessed from the contents of Mrs. Chang's cabin and her jewellery that her husband was extremely rich, but it was accepted that the Chinese should not presume to travel First Class but be accom-modated on a lower deck.

Mr. Chang had, however, engaged three cabins. One was the Sitting-Room, where, while his wife was ill, he sat alone, and there were two bed-room cabins.

When Azalea suggested that she should take Jam Kin into the Sitting-Room so that his mother could go to sleep, Mrs. Chang had been horrified at the idea.

"Jam Kin disturb Honourable husband," she said "Velly important have no noise while work."

Azalea privately thought that Mr. Chang was having a quiet rest by himself, but she did know that a Chinese wife was subservient and self-effacing, and that everything appertaining to her husband's comfort was of more consequence that she or her children.

She therefore thought she would take Jam Kin away from the cabin and play with him in the Saloon.

As they went, moving slowly because it was difficult not to be thrown down by the violence of the ship's tossing, Azalea noticed all the other children playing noisily in the passage.

They were running in and out of their cabins, shouting, screaming, and squabbling with one another.

She started to talk to them and when they gathered round her she told them a story to which they listened with rapt interest.

A Stewardess came by.

"I wondered what was keeping everyone so quiet," she remarked.

"I am afraid we are rather in the way," Azalea said. "Is there a room where we could go?"

Finally the Stewardess had decided that Azalea might use the Writing-Room in the Second Class even though it was against the regulations for the Third-Class children to encroach upon their betters.

"You won't say anything about it, will you, Miss?" the Stewardess asked.

"No, of course not," Azalea answered, and added, "and I hope none of you will mention to my Aunt what I am doing."

She had said the same to the Stewardess on her own deck.

"Don't you worry, Miss, we won't get you into any trouble," the woman answered. "That Soothing Syrup of the Doctor's keeps Her Ladyship so sleepy she wouldn't worry about you even if you were up on the bridge with the Captain!"

"I can assure you that is most unlikely!" Azalea smiled.

She could not help wondering about Lord Sheldon.

She had the feeling that he would not be sea-sick, as everyone else aboard seemed to be.

Once she had opened the door onto the deck because she felt stifled for want of air, and she had seen him leaning in a sheltered spot, watching the waves break over the bow.

She had gone away quickly. She had no desire to see him again, she told herself, and yet when she thought about it she knew that it was not strictly true.

She could not prevent herself from thinking about him and remembering that he had kissed her.

"How can I be so foolish?" she wondered when she was lying awake in the narrow bunk in her small cabin.

Foolish or not, it was impossible to forget what had happened and the feeling he had aroused in her.

Besides, she was honest enough to admit that he was one of the best-looking and most attractive men she had ever seen in her life.

There had been many handsome Officers in the Regiment, and although she had been too young for them to pay any attention to her, she had noticed how well they rode and how fine they looked when they were on parade.

Her father had been good-looking and there had been an irresistible glint of admiration in her mother's eyes when he appeared in full Regimentals or wore his colourful mess-jacket.

"You do look smart, my darling!" Azalea had heard her say once. "There is no-one as fascinating as you!"

"You flatter me!" her father answered. "And you know what I think you look like."

He kissed her mother, but when he had gone Azalea heard her sigh as if she was lonely without him.

"Will I ever fall in love?" Azalea reflected as the *Orissa* rolled creakingly from side to side.

Then as she asked herself the question she remembered her Uncle saying:

"You will never marry!"

That had been two years ago, and she wondered if he still believed that she was so singularly unattractive that it was unlikely that any man would wish to make her his wife.

Azalea knew she had altered. She was not beautiful like her mother—that was impossible! But even though she was dark and not prettily pink and white like the twins, she could not believe there was not a man somewhere in the world who would love her.

Perhaps one day she would find him, and together they would defy her Uncle.

Even to think about it made Azalea tremble.

Sir Frederick was intimidating and she knew that if as her legal Guardian he intended her not to marry, as he had said, she would not be able to do so.

"Mama would have wanted me to be happy," she told herself.

They had talked together of marriage.

"You love Papa very much, do you not, Mama?" she had asked.

"I love him with all my heart and with all my soul, Azalea," her mother replied. "One day you will fall in love, and you will realise, as I did, that money and social position are completely unimportant beside the fact that one is loved and one loves!"

There was something in her mother's voice and the smile on her lips which made Azalea know she had found something very wonderful and very beautiful.

"Love is beauty," she told herself now, "the beauty that I long for, the beauty that I lost when I left India."

Azalea played with the children every afternoon and sometimes in the morning, until gradually the sea grew calmer, the air warmer, and they were through the Straits of Gibraltar and into the Mediterranean.

The grown-up passengers began to recover and the Stewardesses told Azalea that they could no longer allow the children of the Third-Class passengers to come up to the Writing-Room in the Second-Class deck.

Soon she found herself spending any time she was free in Mrs. Chang's cabin and they became friends.

"How I thank you for gracious kindness me and Jam Kin?" Mrs. Chang asked.

"You have been kind to me," Azalea said. "I should have been very lonely if I had not been able to talk to you."

She paused and then she said a little tentatively:

"I wonder if I might ask you something?"

"Please ask," Mrs. Chang replied.

"I want to learn Chinese," Azalea said, "and I do not know how to start about it."

"I teach," Mrs. Chang said.

"No, no! I did not mean that!" Azalea answered quickly. "I would not wish to impose upon you. It is just that I thought you might have a book or something very simple by which I could start to understand the language."

"I talk Mr. Chang. You wait."

Mrs. Chang left Azalea with Jam Kin and after a short while came back to say excitedly:

"Come! Come meet Mr. Chang."

Azalea was only too willing to follow her. She was very anxious to meet Mr. Chang. She had wondered so often what he was like.

Mrs. Chang led her into the Sitting-Room which lay between the two sleeping-cabins.

Seated in a comfortable chair was a Chinese gentleman who looked, Azalea thought, exactly as she might have expected.

He was dressed in an exquisitely embroidered Chinese robe and his feet were enclosed in padded slippers. On his head he wore a small round cap and his queue which fell down his back was thick even though it was nearly white like his beard.

He had a fine face, Azalea thought, but while she had a quick impression of his appearance she was embarrassed as Mrs. Chang went down on her knees and prostrated herself.

"Honourable husband," she said in English, "may humble insignificant wife present kind and honourable English lady."

Mr. Chang rose to his feet and bowed with his hands inside his wide sleeves. Azalea curtseyed even while she was certain that her Aunt would disapprove of her curtseying to a Chinese.

"I understand from my unimportant wife that she and my son Jam Kin are greatly indebted to you, Miss Osmund," he said in almost perfect English.

"It has been a great pleasure, Mr. Chang, to be able to help a little while your wife has been so ill."

"Women are bad sailors," Mr. Chang said. "Will you honour me by sitting down, Miss Osmund, on this inferior and uncomfortable chair?"

It was very Chinese, Azalea knew, to disparage one's own possessions, but she thought the P.&O. might have been somewhat displeased at the description of one of their well-padded arm-chairs.

She seated herself and Mrs. Chang rose from the floor to sit on a low stool.

"My wife tells me that you wish to learn our difficult language," Mr. Chang said.

There was a note in his voice which made Azalea sure he thought it most improbable that she would ever achieve such an ambition.

"I would like to be able to read and also to talk with the people of Hong Kong," Azalea answered. "I am half Russian, so perhaps it will not be as difficult for me as it would be for someone who was completely European."

"You will find it a difficult language," Mr. Chang said. "There are various dialects of Chinese, but Cantonese is most commonly used in Hong Kong."

"Then I would like to learn Cantonese," Azalea said.

"The original Chinese characters were simple hieroglyphics like ancient Egyptian ones."

"They are very beautiful," Azalea said, and she thought, although his expression did not alter, that he was pleased by her praise.

"Miss Osmund teach me speak better English," Mrs. Chang said. "I teach Chinese, if Honourable husband permit."

"I permit!" Mr. Chang said quietly.

After that, two or three times a day Azalea slipped down to the Second-Class deck and into Mrs. Chang's cabin.

She discovered that her name was Kai Yin and she was the third wife of Mr. Chang. She was very accomplished and could embroider and paint exquisitely on silk.

She could make the Chinese characters flow from her hand as she wrote from right to left on the heavy parchment paper her husband had provided for their lessons.

She was child-like in her enjoyment of the ridiculous and she would laugh at the mistakes Azalea made until sometimes she found it so amusing that the tears came into her eyes.

In Chinese it was very easy to make mistakes because every monosyllable had several basic different meanings and everything depended on the inflection of the voice.

Azalea found that *hsing* meant awaken, passionless, anger, rise, punish, apricot, figure, and to blow the nose with the fingers! *Hsing* also meant "sex."

Fortunately Azalea, as she had hoped, did not find it as difficult as an ordinary English girl might have done, and she also had a musical ear.

By the time they had sailed through the Mediterranean Lady Osmund was on her feet again.

No longer under the influence of the Soothing Syrup the Doctor had prescribed, she found dozens of things for Azalea to do for her.

But she had no wish for Azalea to accompany the twins when they walked the deck in the sunshine, or sat in the Saloon gossiping with the other passengers whom Lady Osmund considered of enough social importance.

"I cannot stay long," Azalea said to Mrs. Chang. "My Aunt has given me a dress to mend and some handkerchiefs to embroider. If I stay with you I shall never get them done."

"I help," Mrs. Chang said.

"I could not let you do that," Azalea protested.

"We sew and talk Cantonese," Mrs. Chang insisted.

What had been a boring chore became an amusing one. Besides, Azalea's cabin was so dark that it hurt her eyes to work there for long. It was also very hot.

Sometimes there were so many things that Mrs. Chang wanted to ask about England, and so much Azalea had to tell her, that it was quicker to talk in English, but at other times Mrs. Chang was a strict teacher.

"You say Chinese word," she would order sternly.

Then she would go into peals of laughter as Azalea made some remark with a double entendre that according to Mrs. Chang was quite unrepeatable!

"Your embroidery is certainly improving," Lady Osmund said one evening.

Azalea was so surprised at being praised by her Aunt that for a moment she could find no words with which to reply.

"I had thought that when we reach Hong Kong it might be a good idea for you to take some lessons in embroidery, because it would be cheaper than having to pay the Chinese," Lady Osmund said, "but now I wonder if you really need them."

She then produced quite a number of gowns and underclothes that she wanted either embroidered or appliquéd, and Azalea wondered almost despairingly if she would ever be able to keep up the standard that Mrs. Chang had set for her.

When they went to the Dining-Saloon for meals, Lady Osmund made quite certain that Azalea was not seated anywhere near Lord Sheldon.

There was always either Violet or Daisy beside him,

but he took to coming down later and later to meals, and usually they had finished before he appeared.

Azalea sometimes wondered if it was because he found the twins impossible to talk to, while the man who occupied the chair on his other side was undoubtedly a bore.

One evening, after she was supposed to have gone to bed, Azalea crept up on deck.

She was well aware how reprehensible her Aunt would think her doing such a thing, but the evenings were warm and the sky was filled with stars.

Azalea longed to feel against her cheeks the soft, moist air that they had encountered after reaching the Red Sea.

They had gone ashore at Alexandria and when they rejoined the ship to sail on to Port Said they had seen less and less of Lord Sheldon.

Azalea was sure he was deliberately avoiding Lady Osmund. Unfortunately, her Aunt thought so too, and was extremely cross with the twins.

"Why can you not make yourselves more pleasant?" she asked them. "You had Lord Sheldon sitting next to you at dinner the other evening, Violet, and I notice that you made no effort to converse with him. Why could you not ask him about Hong Kong or India, where he met your father?"

"What should I say, Mama?" Violet asked helplessly.

"Ask him to tell you about the places he has visited," Lady Osmund said in an irritated tone. "Really, what is the point of my spending all this money on elaborate gowns for you both if you do nothing but talk to each other?"

She looked at their pretty, stupid faces and her eyes narrowed for a moment.

"If I have much more nonsense," she said, "and you do not put yourselves out to be ingratiating, I shall send one of you home!"

There was silence for a moment and then the twins cried out simultaneously:

"No, no, Mama! You cannot do that! We cannot be separated!"

"I am half inclined to believe that is the best thing to do," Lady Osmund said. "I shall talk to your father about it."

She swept from the cabin, leaving the twins staring at each other despairingly.

"We cannot be parted—we cannot!" they cried in identical voices and turned to Azalea.

"Mama did not mean it, did she?"

Because she was sympathetic, knowing how much it meant for them to be together, Azalea said:

"You must try when your mother is there to talk and smile at any young man to whom she introduces you."

"I do not mind some men," Daisy said, "but Lord Sheldon frightens me! He is so stiff, and besides he is old!"

"I should think he is about twenty-nine," Azalea said, "Or perhaps thirty. That is not so old, Daisy."

"It is old too me," Daisy retorted, and Azalea felt that that was somehow very true.

Now as she reached the deck she found to her relief that it was empty. Everyone who had not retired to bed was in the Saloon, playing cards, or else in the Smoking-Room where the Bar was situated.

Lady Osmund never went there, but Azalea used to hear laughter and raised voices and thought as she passed the open door that it sounded much the gayest part of the ship.

She went to the rail to lean over it and watch the phosphorus in the water moving away from the ship's side.

It was like a reflection of light from the stars above her head and she looked up, thinking that the sky seemed big and boundless, stretching away into infinity, and having a mystery that she had never noticed when she was in England.

She heard a footstep behind her and knew instinctively without turning her head who was there.

"You are very elusive, Miss Osmund," a voice said, and she thought there was a slightly mocking note in it.

Slowly, because she was shy, she turned to look at him.

She could see his face very clearly in the moonlight and she saw that he was looking at her in that strange, searching way which had seemed characteristic of him ever since she had known him.

"Where do you hide yourself?" he asked. "And I would like you to answer that question."

"Why should it be of interest to you?" Azalea enquired.

"Shall I say I am curious about someone who hides behind curtains and can talk Russian?"

Azalea was suddenly very still.

"H-how did you . . . k-know that?" she asked after a moment.

"Perhaps I should have said that you can sing in Russian."

Azalea realised that he must be aware of the times she had spent with the children.

She did not pretend to misunderstand. Instead she said:

"It was the only song I knew where the children could join in by clapping their hands."

"The Stewardesses are full of your praises."

"They were very overworked during the storm."

"And you are a good sailor?"

"Apparently . . . so."

"I think perhaps you are a very unusual person, Miss Osmund. What else interests you, besides information on Hong Kong, children who need entertaining, and perhaps the Chinese?"

Azalea was very still.

"How did you . . . learn of . . . that?"

"I have ways of finding out what I want to know," Lord Sheldon replied.

Azalea was about to tell him that it was none of his business, when she realised that should he mention to her Aunt what she had been doing, she would be in grave trouble.

After a moment she said in a very low voice:

"Please ... would you say ... nothing to Aunt Emily about this? She would not ... approve. She would be very ... angry."

"You are afraid of her! Why?"

"My parents are dead. My Uncle took me into his ... house but they did not ... want me."

Lord Sheldon rested his arms on the rail and looked out to sea.

"Is it hard to feel unwanted?" he asked surprisingly.

"It is humiliating to be kept out of charity, and not out of affection."

Azalea spoke the truth without thinking. Then she thought she had been indiscreet and looked at him apprehensively.

"You must know that I would never do anything to hurt you," Lord Sheldon said reassuringly, "but are you not running rather grave risks?"

Azalea thought he was referring to her Chinese lessons.

"Papa always thought it most important to be able to converse with people in their own language," she said. "He could always talk to the Indians in Urdu or in several dialects, with the result that they came to him with their troubles and he was able to help them."

"And you want to help the Chinese?" Lord Sheldon asked.

"I want to learn about them, to understand what they think and feel."

Even as she spoke Azalea realised again how indiscreet she had been.

Had she not heard with her own ears Lord Sheldon's sentiments regarding natives when he had talked with Captain Widcombe?

It must be because it was night and he had taken her unawares that she had been so unguarded.

Quickly she tried to cover up her mistake.

"I ... I am speaking about ... reading," she said. "It is unlikely I shall have a chance to ... speak Chinese except perhaps to ... servants."

Lord Sheldon looked at her.

"There is no need for you to be afraid of me," he said quietly.

"I am . . . not!" Azalea replied quickly, and realised that that was not the truth.

She was afraid of him; afraid because he was different from any other man she had ever met; afraid because she told herself she disliked him; and yet he had managed to evoke in her the most wonderful feelings she had ever known.

"Please . . . please," she said hesitatingly, her eyes very large in her small face, "please . . . forget what we have said. Forget that I have spoken to you here tonight. I was not . . . thinking clearly."

"If you are honest you will admit you were speaking the truth," Lord Sheldon said, "and the truth is what I always want to hear."

"Sometimes it is difficult to know what is the truth," Azalea said, thinking of him. "It may seem to be one thing and yet be another."

"Perhaps like the Chinese you seek the world behind the world," Lord Sheldon said.

He saw the question in Azalea's eyes and went on:

"The thought behind the word, the motive behind the action. It is something the Chinese have known and understood since the beginning of their civilisation."

"That is what they try to paint," Azalea said softly.

"And to carve, to think, to feel, and to live," Lord Sheldon said. "They are a very remarkable people."

Azalea looked at him in astonishment.

"You can say that? But you said . . ."

She was about to quote what she had overheard him say to Captain Widcombe.

Then, thinking back over that conversation, she realised for the first time that when he had spoken of "showing white superiority" it had been in answer to Captain Widcombe's question: "What does the War Office think?"

How stupid she had been, she told herself.

Lord Sheldon had been speaking with that mocking note in his voice and she had not realised that he was being sarcastic.

In case she had made a mistake she said tentatively:

"You speak as if you . . . like the Chinese."

"I admire them," Lord Sheldon replied. "Do you re-alise they were printing paper money when we in En-gland were still walking about in woad!"

He paused and then went on:

"The majority of them have high principles, integ-rity, and a strong sense of honour."

Azalea clasped her hands together.

"That is what Mama said, but I thought . . ."

"I know exactly what you thought . . . Miss Os-mund," Lord Sheldon said with a smile. "You made it quite clear at our first meeting."

"I am very sorry," Azalea said. "It was very . . . rude of me."

He did not answer and after a moment she said:

"It was foolish of me to be impetuous, to make up my mind so quickly. But I despise the attitude . . . some people . . . have of looking down contemptuously on people of other Nations."

"I agree with you," Lord Sheldon said quietly.

"Then I can only . . . apologise for having . . . misunderstood what you said when I should not have been . . . listening to your . . conversation."

"You are very disarming, Miss Osmund," Lord Sheldon remarked, "but there are still quite a lot of unanswered questions where you are concerned."

"Why should you . . . think that?" Azalea asked in surprise.

Then it suddenly came to her mind that perhaps he was about to ask her how her father had met his death.

He had been in India, where gossip where a Regi-ment was concerned was passed from one soldier to another and from Bazaar to Bazaar. It might be that something he had heard had made him suspicious.

She knew then that she could not let him ask her any questions of which her Uncle would disapprove.

Sir Frederick had told her that the secret must go with her to the grave, and if either he or her Aunt knew that she had been discovered speaking Russian they would be furiously angry.

In the starlight Azalea looked up into Lord Sheldon's eyes.

They were searching her face in that strange, unaccountable manner they had done before, and quite suddenly he seemed large and overwhelming.

He was very near to her and she wondered if once again he might put his arms round her and kiss her.

If he did so, she thought, if he even touched her, she would be only too willing to tell him anything he wanted to know.

Ever since he had been talking to her she had felt her heart beating frantically within her breast and had been conscious of a strange weakness because he was so near.

Now she saw the danger of it.

She realised how much he had learnt about her already and how easy it would be for him to learn so much more.

And yet it seemed his eyes held her spellbound and she could not escape. Then she thought that his hand went out, although that might have been an illusion.

She made an inarticulate little sound and before he could prevent her she turned and ran away from him as she had run from him once before.

There was the sound of her feet on the deck, the decisive click of a door closing behind her, and Lord Sheldon was alone.

Chapter Four

It seemed incredible to Lord Sheldon that anyone could be so elusive.

He wanted to talk with Azalea—he wanted to go on trying to solve the mystery about her and the secrets which he felt he could almost see hiding in her dark eyes, and yet he could not get near her.

From the moment she had run away from him after they had talked together on deck, she had seemed to vanish.

Lord Sheldon had travelled on many ships and he had found it almost impossible to escape from the importunate women who sought his company and, when possible, his embraces.

He had often cursed because a ship was so small that there was nowhere to hide and he felt like a hunted fox.

But Azalea apparently found it quite easy to avoid him.

He discovered from the steward in the Dining-Saloon that either she had her meals at such irregular hours it was impossible for him to catch her at the table, or she had them sent to her cabin.

He did not realise that Lady Osmund found her a lot of needlework to do and thus deliberately kept Azalea away from the Dining-Saloon, because she wished him to concentrate his attentions either on Violet or Daisy.

During the hot, moist nights when the sky was a panorama of stars and the ship moved slowly through the still waters of the Red Sea and out into the Indian Ocean, Lord Sheldon walked every night round and round the decks, hoping to find Azalea, but in vain.

As he had expected, as soon as the ship reached calmer waters and the parents of the children were no longer sea-sick, Azalea did not need to keep them amused in the Writing-Room of the Second Class.

And yet Lord Sheldon often looked in hopefully, only to find the room occupied by old men playing whist or occasionally a tight-lipped spinster writing home of her experiences on board.

Finally when Hong Kong was only forty-eight hours away Lord Sheldon swallowed his pride and wrote a note to Azalea.

It was very short and when she opened it she found it contained only four words:

I must see you!—S.

Lord Sheldon managed to slip the note under the door of Azalea's cabin when everyone had gone to dinner.

As usual, she was not at the Captain's table, and he noticed that her unoccupied chair had been removed.

All his life Lord Sheldon had been the hunter as well as the hunted.

He might be pursued by women who did not interest him, but when his own desires were aroused he pursued the object of his affections with an ardency and expertise which made him invariably the victor.

Now he found himself uncertain as to what would be the outcome of this particular pursuit.

He waited eagerly and, although he would not admit it to himself, apprehensively for Azalea's reply to his note.

There was nothing in his cabin when he went there after dinner. But very much later that night when he had walked round the deck and waited for a long time in the place where he had talked to Azalea before, he entered his cabin to find a small piece of paper laying on the floor.

It contained one word:

No!

He stared at it for a long time and then his lips tightened.

He had no intention of being defeated.

He, who had tracked down Russian agents in India, who had surmounted innumerable hazards on dangerous journeys including one across the snow-capped mountains of Afghanistan, was not going to be defied by one small dark-eyed girl who had aroused his interest.

"Damnit all!" he told himself. "I will get to the bottom of this if it is the last thing I ever do!"

But the ship was nearing Hong Kong, and he had the feeling that once Azalea was installed at Flagstaff House Lady Osmund was going to prove a prickly barrier to prevent him from contacting her.

The last night aboard Lord Sheldon went down to the Third-Class deck to say good-bye to Mrs. Favel.

She was pathetically grateful for all his kindness.

"I hopes I never has to go to sea again, M'Lord," she said, "and if my husband's sent to any more of these heathenish parts I'll not go with him, and that's a fact!"

"Now, Mrs. Favel," Lord Sheldon said soothingly, "you know as well as I do that the Sergeant Major cannot manage without you, and besides, the children would miss him."

Mrs. Favel protested, though somewhat feebly, and Lord Sheldon was sure that when the time came for her to accompany her husband again she would do her duty.

He gave her some money to buy presents for the children, then climbed the narrow companion-way up to the Second-Class deck.

He actually had his foot on the stairs to go higher, when looking down the passage he saw a figure he recognised come out of a cabin at the far end of it and start walking towards him.

He waited a little while, until he was sure it was Azalea, and then he walked towards her.

Her head was bowed and she was obviously deep in thought, so that she did not see him until she actually looked up to find him barring her way.

She gave a little gasp of surprise.

"I have been trying to see you."

"I . . . I have been . . . busy."

"Why are you avoiding me?"

She was about to say that she was not doing so, when as she looked into his face the lie died on her lips.

"We have a lot to say to each other, Azalea," he said quietly, and she did not realise that he had used her Christian name for the first time.

"I . . . have . . . to pack."

"I am certain that has been done already," Lord Sheldon replied, "and anyway it is of little consequence. How can I see you when we reach Hong Kong?"

"You cannot!" she answered. "My Aunt would not allow it, and . . . anyway, I do not wish to . . . see you!"

"Is that the truth?" he asked.

Despite her resolution not to do so Azalea found herself looking into his eyes.

Once again she felt that strange weakness because he was so near her; because he was so large and overpowering and it was impossible to escape him.

She had an uneasy feeling too that she did not really wish to do so.

Then she told herself frantically that the one thing she wanted more than anything else was to be free of him. Yet it was impossible to move and almost impossible to breathe.

His eyes were on hers and once again she felt as if he hypnotised her and was drawing her to him although he had not moved.

Even before his arms went round her she felt as though her whole being melted into his. Then it semed as if without the conscious volition of their wills, without either of them being aware of what was happening, she was close against him and his lips were on hers.

He kissed her as he had done before when they had been in the Study, and yet now his lips were more demanding, more insistent, so that it seemed to Azalea that he completely possessed her and she was no longer herself, but part of him.

Now it was not a warm tide that flowed from her heart to her breast and from her breast to her throat. It was rather a fire, a streak of lightning, something which burned and flamed until it ended against his lips and became part of the fire within him.

How long they stood there Azalea had no idea.

The ship had disappeared. There was not even the sound of the engines—only a music which seemed to come from within herself and yet be part of the whole world.

Nothing else existed; nothing else remained, except the wonder he evoked in her, a feeling of ecstasy which was in fact divine.

As she felt his arms tighten about her there was a sudden chatter of voices, masculine laughter, and a party of passengers came noisily from the Saloon.

Slowly, reluctantly, as if he could not bear to let her go, Lord Sheldon took his arms from Azalea until as the passengers reached them he released her.

They separated to stand back on either side of the passage as the people passed them, looking curiously at Lord Sheldon as they did so.

There must have been over a dozen of them and by the time they had filed by, the women lifting the trains of their long skirts, the men with their hands in their trouser pockets, Azalea had vanished!

Lord Sheldon caught one last glimpse of her gown as she ran up the stairs which led to the First-Class deck, and although he started to walk quickly down the passage after her he knew that it was too late.

The *Orissa* sailed into Victoria Harbour early in the morning and for the first time Azalea saw Hong Kong.

She had learnt all she could about it from Mrs. Chang, from a history-book she had found in the ship's

Library, and from the answers her Uncle condescended
to give to her questions.

She knew that Hong Kong was first occupied by the
British in 1841 and legally ceded to them in perpetuity
by the Emperor of China two years later.

Lord Palmerston, who was Foreign Secretary at the
time, had considered the occupation "utterly prema-
ture." In fact, he dismissed Hong Kong as "a barren island with hardly a house on it."

Queen Victoria, however, thought it a joke, and
wrote to her Uncle, King Leopold of the Belgians, saying:

> *Albert is so much amused at my having got
> the island of Hong Kong, and we think Vic-
> toria ought to be called Princess Hong Kong
> in addition to Princess Royal!*

The history of the eighteen-year Opium War with
China made complex and dry reading with its refer-
ences to the difficulties of British Administration in
curbing the traffic in and addition to drugs.

But nothing Azalea had read, heard, or expected
prepared her for the beauty of the island which she
had heard the General call disparagingly "a pimple on
the backside of China!"

The *Orissa* moved slowly to the anchorage and she
saw why the name Hong Kong meant "Fragrant Harbour."

On the sparklingly gold sea there were innumerable
Chinese junks of every size, their brown sails ribbed
like bats' wings. There were also dhows, ferries, fishing
boats, and trading ships from all over the world.

The water-front buildings were vaguely Italian in the
style common to all European settlements in China.

Pale sienna in colour, they seemed almost to be
drawn in pencil, like the slab of the peak towering
above them which was tawny and brown, while lower
down there was a riot of colour which made Azalea
draw in her breath.

She knew from Mrs. Chang's description that she

was seeing the frangipani trees with their creamy waxen temple-flower blosoms and beneath them the crimson, purple, and gold of azaleas.

A Military launch was sent to the *Orissa* as soon as she anchored to convey Lady Osmund and her party ashore.

An Aide-de-Camp, resplendent in his white uniform, introduced himself and escorted them with much respectful pomp to the launch.

They were rowed ashore under the envious eyes of the less fortunate passengers lining the decks.

"The General deeply regrets, My Lady, that he is unable to welcome you himself," the Aide-de-Camp said respectfully, "but, as you will understand, he has been excessively busy since he arrived."

"I imagined that he would be," Lady Osmund said graciously. "Where is Sir Frederick at this moment?"

"I believe he is with the Governor, Sir John Pope-Hennessey," the Aide-de-Camp replied. "They are having a series of meetings which start early and go on late."

"I am sure that my husband has a great deal to discuss with Sir John," Lady Osmund said.

On the Quayside itself there were the picturesque Chinese Azalea had wanted to see in their large coolie hats, and below on the water, rocking a little in the waves caused by the launch, there were innumerable small sampans, in which, she had learnt, whole families lived and died.

There was a carriage waiting for them drawn by two horses, but Azalea's eyes were on the rickshaws. She was listening too for the first time to the strange, tinkling lilt of the Cantonese language and pidgin English which contained no *r*'s, as the rickshaw-boys solicited clients, crying:

"Lickshaw! Lickshaw!"

As they drove from the wharf the streets were so narrow and so full of pedestrians that it seemed impossible that the horses would find their way through them.

There were many soldiers and sailors and Portuguese Priests and Nuns, and Azalea caught a glimpse of a scarlet-curtained palanquin swaying as it was carried by four sturdy men.

She also saw several Mandarins riding in rickshaws, whom she recognised because they had jade hat-buttons and robes of brilliant satin embroidered with gold thread.

In contrast, there were all too many ragged children staring hungrily at the food-hawkers and at the Chinese who could afford it sitting down in the street for their *shik-an-chan*. Azalea knew this meant their midday meal.

Fish with open mouths and large eyes hung decoratively head-down from the top of open stalls. Red snappers caught off Hainan; Sea bream, which had red swelling between their eyes; Lizard fish with mouths entirely lined with teeth; Macao sole and the huge Conger pike with dagger-like teeth and smooth, tapering bodies.

Mrs. Chang had taught Azalea about these and also about the birds of Hong Kong, many of which she could see for sale in gold-painted cages.

The yellow-green South China Whale-Eye seemed to be a favourite with the small shop-keepers.

"Gay bird cheer up sad people," Mrs. Chang had explained.

"You mean shop-keepers have cages of them just to please their customers?" Azalea asked.

"Happy customers buy more," Mrs. Chang replied.

The bird Azalea wanted most to see was the Chinese Blue Magpie. Mrs. Chang had described and even drawn for her the Magpie's dazzling blue wings and tail, his coral-red bill and legs.

"We believe to see a Blue-bird brings luck," Azalea explained.

"Many Blue Magpies—you much good luck!" Mrs. Chang smiled.

"I hope so," Azalea said wistfully, thinking, however that it was unlikely.

She had the uneasy feeling that once she reached Flagstaff House she would once again become a household maid-of-all-trades, incessantly abused and criticised by her Aunt.

There were crowds everywhere. Never had Azalea imagined that so many people could be jammed into such a small space.

Every house seemed to be tottering and bending under the weight of the human life within it.

The air was full of cries and voices, the clop-clop of wooden shoes, and the smell of spicy cooking.

'It is just as I expected it would be!' Azalea thought.

But she had not realised that the streets would be so beautiful with long, narrow, coloured pennants and banners hanging from the high houses.

In the richer parts, balconies were festooned with creepers, while the houses with their porticos and colonades looked cool in the hot sunshine which seemed to come from an almost purple sky.

"Really, the place smells!" Lady Osmund said sharply as they passed what looked like a huge perambulator on which a Chinese man was cooking several different dishes at the same time.

No-one answered her and after a moment, as if determined to find fault, she said:

"The coolies look ridiculous with their enormous hats like overturned basins!"

Azalea longed to answer that she thought the coolies made everything seem Oriental and exciting. But she knew that such a remark would only be replied to contemptuously by her Aunt and therefore refrained from speaking.

Flagstaff House was, she thought, like every other important British residence abroad. She had seen so many of them in India, and they all appeared to have been designed on the same pattern.

Solid, imposing, they were unmistakably English, just as the rooms inside might have been conveyed there complete in every detail from Camberley, Aldershot, Cheltenham, or Bournemouth.

There were the same polished mahogany chairs and flowered chintz cutrains over the windows; the same badly executed oleographs of the Quen and the Prince

Consort; the same second-quality Persian rugs; and outside, the same effort to create an English garden.

There were pansies, wall flowers, marigolds, asters, and forget-me-nots planted in tiny beds and chosen by every General's wife to remind her of home.

"Now, Azalea," Lady Osmund said sharply, "you had better see to the unpacking."

"There are a number of Chinese servants in the house, My Lady," the Aide-de-Camp said quickly, "and more can be procured, if you will let me know your requirements."

"My niece can supervise them," Lady Osmund said. "That is what she does at home, and it will keep her occupied."

The way in which her Aunt spoke the words made it clear to Azalea that she was determined to keep her busy, however many servants were employed at Flagstaff House.

Fortunately, as soon as Lady Osmund had settled in she discovered a dozen things she needed from the shops. Too busy socially to go herself, she ordered Azalea to buy her what was required.

As she was of no importance, an elderly Chinese servant, who like the rest was traditionally called "boy," was deputed to be her guide.

Azalea asked his name and was told it was Ah Yok.

She knew that the twins would have been escorted by an Aide-de-Camp and conveyed in a carriage, but she was only too content to go with Ah Yok in two rickshaws.

In fact, she preferred it.

They set out and Azalea realised that Ah Yok was taking her to the shops in the Old Praya, patronised by the English.

In her somewhat halting Chinese she explained what she wanted and there was a faint smile on Ah Yok's wide mouth as he commanded the rickshaw-boys to convey them further into the town.

Azalea soon insisted on discarding the rickshaws and walking in streets so narrow and so over-hung with signs that they excluded the sun, and up the flights of steep steps to visit the real Chinese quarters which Mrs. Chang had described to her.

There were little bread-shops which sold delicious freshly baked *yeh see min bao,* which were rolls with sweet grated coconut in the centre of them.

There were stalls with fruits piled in polychromatic pyramids of colour, and the *Min Yan* who made for the children tiny coloured toys—tigers, cats, dogs, and ducks—out of flour paste.

The noise of the hawkers and peddlers, crying salted fish, brooms, incense, and blood gelatin, rang in Azalea's ears. Ah Yok explained that they had to buy wooden tickets for fifty cents which entitled them to call their wares.

Some of them carried large, flat rattan cages containing *um chun*—timid little brown birds called quail. Others cried *um chun don,* which were tiny little quails' eggs—much favoured in Chinese soups.

In one street packed with children Azalea found the blind musicians singing and playing *Nan Yin.* One musician played the *ts'in-hu*—a violin with a twelve-inch-space soundbox, while another worked the *p'ai-pan,* or clappers, with one hand and strummed the *ku-cheng,* or Chinese zither, with the other.

"Velly old music," Ah Yok explained. "First mentioned Sung Dynasty."

Whatever Azalea bought was recorded on a wooden abacus, a calculator which had been invented, she learnt from the guide-book, by Chhiwhuni-Wen, a metallurgist, nearly a thousand years previously.

Like a child's toy, the beads were pushed backwards and forwards so swiftly by the thin, sensitive Chinese fingers that the total seemed to be calculated by magic.

What fascinated Azalea were the Medicine-Shops with the rows of square bottles, their dried sea-horses from the warm Gulf of Tonkin, and bears' galls from the Tibetan highlands.

"Vipers from jungles of Kwangi," Ah Yok pointed out. "Deers' antlers from Manchurian forests."

Azalea had been told by Mrs. Chang that these were to ensure a long life and for their aphrodisiac properties were as prized as the wild Manchurian Ginseng, which had been believed for centuries to cure all disease.

"Some herbs five thousand years old," Ah Yok said proudly in Chinese, and the shop-keeper nodded agreement and showed Azalea herbs for rectifying the heat of "high fever" and for "purging the fire."

Azalea had read that the Chinese believed there were two opposing principles in nature, *Yin* and *Yang,* disease being a manifestation of unbalance in the body; health, of balance and harmony.

The shop-keeper confirmed this:

"The heart, husband," he said, "lungs, wife."

"What he is saying," Ah Yok explained, "if no harmony between two—evil arises!"

Azalea was shown the famous tonics of the Galens of China, which included stalactite, dried lizard skins which were red and spotted, dog flesh, human milk, teeth of dragons, and shavings of rhinoceros horns.

Even though she found it hard to believe in the efficacy of such treatments, it was absorbingly interesting, and only with the utmost reluctance did she allow Ah Yok to take her back to Flagstaff House.

"Thank you, Ah Yok, thank you very much," she said when they arrived.

"Great privilege, Honourable Lady," Ah Yok said with sincerity, and Azalea knew she had found a friend.

One of the first things Azalea learnt in Hong Kong concerned Lord Sheldon.

She had found it impossible after leaving the *Orissa* to decide to herself what she thought about him.

She had been bewildered and confused by her own emotions when he had kissed her the second time, and she had run away from him to lock herself in her cabin and throw herself down on her bunk, quivering with emotions she had not known she possessed.

"Why should he kiss me? Why should he want to?" she asked, and could find no answer.

She could not really believe that he was attracted to her. How could he be?

When they had met first in such strange circumstances, she knew how unattractive she must have looked in the clothes that did not suit her and which had belonged to Violet or Daisy.

And yet his lips had held a compelling magic and she had been lifted by his kiss into a world of wonder and glory. But she could not believe that he could feel the same.

How could he, with his experience, with his title, his importance, his position in the social world?

Azalea was well aware, even without overhearing what Lord Sheldon had said to Captain Widcombe, that any Army Officer who was reasonably good-looking was sought out and flattered.

And if, as in Lord Sheldon's case, he should be coming into a title, he would only have to look in the direction of a woman for her to fall only too eagerly into his arms.

Why then should he trouble to kiss her?

She could not explain it.

Alone in the darkness of her cabin, she admitted to herself that he had given her something to remember in the long years that lay ahead.

At least she would not be ignorant of what a kiss was like, and if the thought of the ecstasy she had experienced made her long for more, then one had always to pay for one's happiness.

Her mother had told her that.

"Nothing is for free, my dearest," she had said once to Azalea. "If one receives, one must also give, and one pays for everything in some way or another—sometimes with an aching heart!"

Azalea had known that her mother was not speaking of herself but of some of the wives in the Regiment who had come to her weeping bitter tears because their husbands were unfaithful.

It was a side of love which Azalea had hoped she would never experience, but now she was not sure.

It was better, she thought, to have been kissed by Lord Sheldon and to know the wonder and joy of it than to go through life as her Uncle intended her to

do, unaware of the rapture one could experience from
a man's touch.

And yet it was hard to tell herself that she would
never see him again.

She knew that he had called the day after they had
landed, but there had been no question of her meeting
him.

Lady Osmund had made it quite clear the moment
they arrived at Flagstaff House that Azalea was to be
kept in the background.

But even to hear his name made something vibrate
and come to life within her.

Her Uncle said on the second day at luncheon when
the family was alone:

"I am disappointed in Sheldon!"

"Disappointed?" Lady Osmund asked. "Why?"

"I believed he had come out here to help put matters straight where the Governor is concerned, but as
far as I can ascertain, he is doing nothing of the sort."

"What can you mean?" Lady Osmund enquired.

"What I say," the General remarked crossly, "is that
he appears to be agreeing with Sir John."

"I cannot believe it!" Lady Osmund exclaimed.
"You must be mistaken!"

The General was scowling and was obviously turning
over in his mind something that had occurred.

"What makes you think that Lord Sheldon is taking
the Governor's side?" Lady Osmund enquired.

"We were discussing at the meeting this morning the
custom prevailing amongst the Chinese community in
Hong Kong of buying and selling girls for the purpose
of making them domestic servants."

"A very sensible custom!" Lady Osmund remarked.

"That is what I thought," the General replied, "but
the Governor is trying to put a stop to it."

"How ridiculous! Why should he interfere?" Lady
Osmund enquired.

"He alleges, I think wrongly, that the kidnapping of
young Chinese girls for exportation to the Straits Settlements and to California and Australia has increased
enormously."

"Had he any evidence of this?"

"He has persuaded the Chief Justice to declare that there is no distinction between the sale of girls for domestic servitude and exportation for immoral purposes."

"I am sure that is nonsense!" Lady Osmund asserted.

"That is what General Donovan said also. But the Chief Justice echoed what the Governor affirmed last year, that there are ten thousand to twenty thousand females slaves in Hong Kong and that this form of slavery flourishes only through the failure of the Government's Officers to enforce the existing laws."

"It sounds very exaggerated to me," Lady Osmund commented.

"That is exactly what I said myself," the General answered. "I have asked for reports on this subject, because it is a matter not only for the police but also for the Military. But one can hardly believe that the whole dispute is to be referred to the Secretary of State in England."

"On whose request?" Lady Osmund enquired.

"Need you ask?" the General replied harshly. "The Governor insisted and was backed up by Lord Sheldon."

"It cannot be true!" Lady Osmund exclaimed.

"As you well know," the General went on, "we have been instructed that every care must be taken not to interfere with the habits and institutions of the Chinese, and this matter of buying for adoption is deeply interwoven into their social customs."

"Perhaps you should speak privately to Lord Sheldon," Lady Osmund suggested. "He is young and I have heard that the Governor can be very persuasive regarding his wild-cat ideas. Surely he must realise that this sort of attitude can be dangerous to the peace and harmony of the whole Colony?"

"I spoke on the subject in no uncertain terms," the General replied. "I am convinced that the Chief Justice is wildly exaggerating the whole matter, while the Governor is inclined to twist anything in which he takes an interest."

"Personally I find him very charming," Lady Osmund said.

"He can be when it suits him. At the same time, I can assure you, my dear, he is a trouble-maker. He never leaves well alone and sooner or later finds himself at variance with every public figure with whom he works!"

The General paused and added somewhat spitefully:

"Sheldon will soon find that he is backing the wrong horse!"

"All the same, Frederick, I think it would be a good idea if you asked Lord Sheldon to dinner this week. I thought when he called yesterday he was being particularly attentive to Daisy."

"If you are considering him in the light of a potential son-in-law," the General said, rising from the table, "I advise you to do nothing of the sort."

"But why, Frederick? Why should you say that?" Lady Osmund asked.

"Because, as I have told you, Sheldon is encouraging the Governor in the very attitude that I am trying to oppose."

"What is that?" Lady Osmund asked.

"His determination to treat the Chinese with an equality to which they have no right."

"An equality?" Lady Osmund echoed, her voice rising.

"That is what I said," the General said firmly. "Do you know what the Governor is called by the Chinese?"

He did not wait for his wife to answer but said contemptuously:

"'Number-One Good Friend'! That shows you the type of man he is!"

The General left the Dining-Room, and Azalea, following Lady Osmund, felt as if her head were in a whirl.

She might have known, she thought, that Lord Sheldon could be none of the things she had first thought about him.

How, if he had been, could he have aroused in her anything so beautiful or so wonderful as the rapture she felt when their lips met?

'How stupid I was!' Azalea thought.

She felt herself blush as she remembered all the accusations she had made to him and how she had told herself how much she hated and despised Lord Sheldon even while she knew that it was untrue.

She did not sleep that night for wondering if she would ever have the chance of telling him again how sorry she was to have misunderstood what he had said to Captain Widcombe.

It would not matter to him, she thought, what she felt about him. At the same time, it was humiliating to know how wrong she had been and how foolish.

Because she felt perturbed and so upset after what her Uncle had said, she could not settle down to sew after Lady Osmund and the twins left in an open carriage for Government House.

The Governor was giving a garden-party and all the most fashionable people in Hong Kong were to be present.

The party set off without saying good-bye to her and she stood a little forlornly in the Hall, conscious that the Aides-de-Camp who accompanied Lady Osmund had glanced at her in a somewhat embarrassed manner.

They had learnt by this time her position in the household, and that even the smallest efforts on their part to be polite to her were frowned upon both by the General and his wife.

Azalea walked upstairs to her bed-room to stand for a moment looking out over the trees towards the blue water in the Bay and beyond it to Kowloon.

The sunshine seemed to glitter like gold, and yet there was a darkness within herself which overshadowed the joy of being warm again.

It was then that she made up her mind.

She had promised Mrs. Chang that she would go to visit her, and this was her opportunity not only to see someone she thought of as a friend but also to have a lesson in Chinese.

"Come anytime!" Mrs. Chang had said. "You always welcome in my husband's house."

Bravely, because she knew that if it was discovered her Aunt would be furious, Azalea put on her hat and, taking a small lace-trimmed sunshade which had once belonged to one of the twins, went downstairs and asked for a rickshaw.

A servant summoned one to the door and she got into it, feeling that it was an adventure to be pulled swiftly down the drive of Flagstaff House and out into the road.

The rickshaw-boy had bare feet and his clothes were ragged. But he hummed a tune as he ran, and Azalea had the feeling that he was happy.

Mr. Chang's house was, Azalea knew, a little way up the side of the peak above the elegant white houses built by the Europeans in Victoria.

When they reached it she saw with delight that it was completely Chinese with its green tiles and carved eaves ornamented with porcelain dragons.

She paid the rickshaw-boy, knowing that she would not be able to afford to keep him waiting for her, and was bowed into the house, which was built Chinese-fashion round several court-yards.

It was, Azalea saw, a very impressive and luxurious residence even for a rich Chinese.

Kai Yin Chang was delighted to see her.

"You honour us with your presence," she said, bowing almost to the ground; then, forgetting ceremony, she clapped her hands to exclaim:

"I hope you come! I much to say! You very welcome!"

Azalea saw her apartments and felt she could have spent hours looking at the long, scroll-like Chinese pictures on the walls, the pottery which she knew was very old, and the exquisitely carved pieces of jade.

Never had Azalea imagined that jade could range in colour from pure white through clear emerald-green to dark, almost black, green.

There was a Neophrite dish of warm bronze exquisitely carved with feline figures.

"Chow Dynasty," Mrs. Chang told her.

A carving of a flowering lotus was in white and pale green, so delicately executed that Azalea felt she could almost see the petals move.

"Ch'ing Dynasty," Mrs. Chang said.

Most elaborate was a white jade bottle ornamented with rubies and emeralds in a gold setting, but Azalea preferred a coral carving of Wang Mu riding above the clouds.

"Honourable husband say jade come from Heaven, heals body and gives immortality," Mrs. Chang said in Chinese.

"I am not certain I want to live forever," Azalea replied, "but I would love to own even a tiny piece."

"Jade also keep away evil thoughts," Mrs. Chang went on. "Bring plenty good luck."

"Then I must certainly try to possess a small piece," Azalea said wistfully.

She looked at the jade again, feeling almost as if it had the power to help her.

"What wonderful pieces Mr. Chang has collected!" she exclaimed.

"He buy many, many, some he sell, some he keep. Best he keep for home."

Azalea was sure that that was true, but she found that Kai Yin Chang knew really very little about them or their value. She only liked, as do women of every Nation, to have beautiful things round her.

An Ayah brought in Jam Kin, looking attractively doll-like, and then he was taken away for a rest.

"What we do?" Kai Yin Chang asked.

"Please show me more of your wonderful possessions," Azalea begged. "They are so exciting for me."

"Show you my clothes," Kai Yin Chang replied.

She brought from cupboards and chests the most exquisitely embroidered tunics that Azalea had ever seen. To go with them were trousers in brilliant coloured satin, and coats for the winter were lined with sable and rich furs.

Kai Yin Chang was wearing a tunic of dark emerald-green with trousers of orange satin. When she left the house and on formal occasions she wore a petticoat which was a straight square of embroidery in the front and at the back, and open at the sides. This was richly embroidered like a Mandarin's robe.

"What do you wear under your tunic?" Azalea asked.

"Very little! You try one . . . very comfortable."

Azalea hesitated, but there was something fascinating in the thought of trying on anything so beautiful.

Kai Yin Chang chose for her a tunic of deep rose-pink embroidered with flowers of many colours.

It was lined and piped at the neck and down the sides of the slits with a pale leaf-green, and as soon as Azalea put it on she realised what a difference the colour made to her skin and to the lights in her hair.

Now she realised how pastel shades, which were so becoming to Violet and Daisy, made her seem sallow and took away from her natural colouring.

It seemed very daring to put on the satin trousers which matched the lining of the tunic and were turned up with rose-pink.

They made her feel how large her feet were compared with Kai Yin Chang's. She, like all Chinese women, had had her feet bound as a child.

Kai Yin Chang had told her about it when they were on the *Orissa*.

"Only slave girls not bound," she had said.

Azalea had listened in horror to the details. At eight years of age, when the bones of a girl's foot have become sufficiently hardened to bear the incessant pressure—the binding begins.

The pain was excruciating, the discomfort was actual torture, to be effective in contracting the feet into such a small compass that they would fit into a shoe of two to three inches in length.

"I scream, cry, all day—all night!" Kai Yin Chang said almost proudly.

"When did the pain stop?" Azalea asked.

"Three—four years!" Kai Yin Chang answered. "But Honourable husband think feet beautiful!"

"You are very brave!" Azalea said, but Kai Yin Chang only smiled.

"Now wear hair like me," she said, to change the subject.

She let down Azalea's long hair and tied it with a pink ribbon and decorated it with hair-pins which had beautiful carved green tops.

"You very beautiful!" she exclaimed. "I lend ear-rings."

It was such fun dressing up, and Azalea could hardly believe the difference the Chinese dress made to her appearance.

"You best in bold Chinese colours, not milky ones," Kai Yin Chang said, and they both laughed.

When Azalea stood up she realised that she and Kai Yin Chang did in fact look very much alike.

"Two Chinese girls!" Kai Yin Chang said, as if she read Azalea's thoughts. "No-one think you English!"

"I am very happy to be Chinese," Azalea smiled.

There was a sudden light of mischief in Kai Yin Chang's eyes.

"We play joke on Mr. Chang," she said. "I introduce you as Chinese friend."

"No! We had better not!" Azalea cried quickly, but she was too late.

Kai Yin Chang had run from the room. When she returned she said:

"Servants say Honourable husband in room. Come with me. We surprise him!"

She drew Azalea by the hand and because she did not want to spoil Kai Yin Chang's excitement she did not protest.

They ran across the court-yard and into another part of the house, which, Azalea saw, contained even more wonderful treasures than those in Kai Yin Chang's apartments.

There was a servant standing outside Mr. Chang's room, the door of which was made of black walnut, or-namented with magnificent gold carving.

He opened it, and Kai Yin Chang moved forward, pulling Azalea by the hand.

"You make obeisance like me," she whispered.

Inside the room, she sank down onto her knees, putting her head on her outstretched hands. Azalea did the same.

"Honourable husband, I beg permission to introduce Honourable friend," she heard Kai Yin Chang say.

"You have my permission, wife," Mr. Chang replied.

Azalea glanced sideways, out of the corner of her eye, at Kai Yin Chang.

She was raising just her head and then her body until she was kneeling on the ground.

Azalea followed her example.

Then as she looked a little shyly at Mr. Chang, wondering if he would immediately penetrate her disguise, she realised he was not alone.

Sitting beside him on a carved ebony chair was Lord Sheldon!

Chapter Five

For a moment Azalea was unable to move, then frantically she hoped that Lord Sheldon would not recognise her.

But Mr. Chang saw immediately that his wife was playing a trick on him.

He rose to his feet and bowed to Azalea.

"It is a very great honour for you to enter my humble house," he said. "Whether you come as Miss Osmund or as 'Fragrant Flower' you are always welcome!"

Azalea was suddenly very conscious of her Chinese dress and that Lord Sheldon was staring at her in his penetrating manner which always made her blush.

Before she could speak, Kai Yin Chang exclaimed in mock exasperation:

"You guessed! You guessed who she was! Honourable husband too clever to be deceived! Very disappointing!"

Azalea would have withdrawn from the room, but as she turned away, embarrassed and uncertain of herself, Lord Sheldon said to Mr. Chang:

"I wonder if it would be possible for me to speak alone with Miss Osmund?"

"But of course, My Lord," Mr. Chang replied. "My house is yours!"

"I am sure Miss Osmund would like to see your beautiful garden," Lord Sheldon said. "And so should I. It is, I am told, one of the sights of Hong Kong."

"You are very gracious," Mr. Chang replied.

Leading the way, he made a gesture to invite Azalea to follow him.

There was nothing she could do but obey. At the same time, she longed to run away—to hide—to change back into her own clothes, and most of all not to have to talk to Lord Sheldon alone.

Yet she was well aware that to argue or protest would merely make her appear ridiculous and would insult him quite unnecessarily in front of Mr. and Mrs. Chang.

She therefore followed her host across another beautiful court-yard and along a passage until they reached a door which led out into the garden.

Mr. Chang opened the door and Azalea and Lord Sheldon walked onto a verandah beyond which lay the garden.

As they appeared they disturbed a number of birds moving about on the grass. They rose as one flock into the air and there was a dazzling glimpse of blue feathers.

"The Blue Magpies!" Azalea exclaimed.

"Let us hope they bring us luck," Lord Sheldon said.

Azalea smiled, remembering what she had said about them on the ship to Mrs. Chang. Then she said almost beneath her breath:

"I need luck!"

They walked side by side down a twisting path edged with sweet-scented flowers.

Azalea had read that Chinese gardens were unusual because of their unique, unsurpassed landscaping.

She had been told that even a small and uninteresting piece of ground could by skilful arrangement be given an impression of space and beauty. But in a large acreage on the side of the peak, Mr. Chang had created a poem of imaginative delight.

There were clever groupings of rock-work, high bridges over ponds covered with water-lilies, small streams and cascades which produced an element of surprise.

The flowers and shrubs were arranged in a harmony and colour that was almost indescribable.

Roses, hydrangeas, peonies, and azaleas, many of the dwarf variety, made a carpet of colour on the ground, while creepers of every hue hung from the boughs of trees and from the eaves of exquisite little pavilions.

Apricot, peach, and orange blossom gave the garden a fairy-like quality and the magnolia trees were pure white against the blue of the sky.

"It is lovely! More lovely than any other garden I can imagine!" Azalea exclaimed.

They had moved a little way from the house to stand looking at the pink-and-white water-lilies on the silver surface of a pond.

"It is very beautiful!" Lord Sheldon agreed, "and so are you in your Chinese costume!"

She looked at him in surprise because the compliment was unexpected; then, seeing the expression in his eyes, she looked quickly away again.

She was trembling.

"I have to see you, Azalea," Lord Sheldon said. "You must realise that."

"It is . . . impossible!"

"But why? Why must you go on pretending that there is nothing between us?"

"There can be nothing!"

"Why? Why? Ever since I have known you, Azalea, you have presented me with insoluble problems, with questions to which I do not know the answers. It cannot go on!"

There was silence for a moment while Azalea clasped her fingers together, her eyes on the water-lilies.

"Your skin is like a magnolia!" Lord Sheldon said. "I know now what was puzzling me about you before."

He paused, but as Azalea did not speak he went on:

"It is because you wear clothes of the wrong colours. The pink of that tunic gives you purple lights in your hair and makes your skin as beautiful as the petal of a flower."

"You should not . . . say such . . . things to . . . me," Azalea answered in a low voice.

"Why not?" he enquired. "Why should I not say what any other man would say if he had the chance?"

"Because I must not . . . listen. You know that my Uncle and Aunt would disapprove."

"I am quite certain they would disapprove much more of your being here alone with me in a garden belonging to a Chinese gentleman," Lord Sheldon said with a hint of laughter in his voice.

"They are my friends," Azalea said as if he challenged her.

"You could not have chosen better," Lord Sheldon answered. "Mr. Chang is a very remarkable man. I had heard about him when he was in England and he was one of the first people upon whom I wished to call when I reached Hong Kong. However, we met first on the *Orissa*."

"Why did you wish to meet him?" Azalea asked because she was curious.

"I wanted Mr. Chang's opinion on how the Colony is run," Lord Sheldon replied, "on the reforms that the Government is trying to put into practice, but most of all I needed his help personally."

He saw the surprise in Azalea's eyes and smiled.

"You are not the only person who admires Chinese beauty. I wish to add jade and pottery to my collection of paintings. There is no-one here more knowledgeable than Mr. Chang."

"I saw some of his treasures in Mrs. Chang's apartments. They were even more exciting than I thought they would be."

"You must get Mr. Chang to tell you the history of some of the pieces he owns," Lord Sheldon said. "And perhaps one day I will be able to tell you about mine."

There was a note in his voice which made Azalea quiver as if she vibrated to strange music, then she said quickly:

"That is . . . something that will never . . . happen. I must be frank with you, My Lord . . . and tell you that we can . . . never even be . . . friends."

"Why not?"

The question was sharp.

"Because my Aunt would never allow it, and you have already offended my Uncle by supporting the Governor."

She made a little gesture with her hands.

"That is immaterial where I am concerned, but for reasons I cannot tell you I am not allowed to have even an acquaintance with any ... man ... let alone you."

"Why me particularly?"

"Because you are too grand ... too important. But even if you were not ... I should be kept ... away from you. As you must realise by this time, I may play no ... part in my Aunt's ... social life."

"I am well aware of that," Lord Sheldon answered. "I instructed the Governor's secretary to be quite certain that you were invited to the garden-party this afternoon. When your Aunt refused on your behalf I guessed you would seize the opportunity to visit your friend Mrs. Chang."

"You came here to look for me?" Azalea asked in astonishment.

"It was one reason, and the most important one, for my visiting Mr. Chang for the second time since my arrival."

Azalea said nothing and after a moment Lord Sheldon continued:

"Look at me, Azalea!"

It was a command and although she wished to disobey him she found herself unable to do so.

Then as she turned her head to look up into his face she could see him silhouetted bare-headed against the pink blossom of an almond tree. It seemed to give him an almost magical appearance.

There was something different about him from other men, she told herself.

It was not his good looks, it was not his air of distinction or authority; it was something else, something that she knew the Chinese would have found when they looked beneath the surface.

"Can you really believe, Azalea," Lord Sheldon asked in his deep voice, "That we can walk away from each other and forget what our lips have said not in words but in a kiss?"

Azalea felt the colour come into her cheeks and she could not take her eyes from his.

"It is . . . what we . . . have to do," she whispered.

"Tell me why. Tell me the truth, Azalea."

"I cannot. It is not my . . . secret."

"Secrets! Secrets!" Lord Sheldon cried with a note of anger in his voice. "You surround yourself with them, and yet I am convinced there is no necessity for them. No-one's eyes could be so innocent or so pure and hide anything of which they need feel ashamed."

Azalea gave a little sigh.

He put his hands on her shoulders and turned her round to face him.

"Tell me what you are hiding. I have to know."

Azalea shook her head.

"It is something I can never tell . . . anyone, least of all . . . you."

"Do you really think you can silence me with such a statement?" he enquired. "I shall find out the truth, Azalea."

"No!" she cried, and twisting herself out of his hold she said violently:

"Leave me alone! There is nothing you can find out . . . nothing you will learn. Nothing! Just go away and forget about me!"

"And will you forget me?"

She wanted to answer him defiantly but it was impossible. The words stuck in her throat. She knew she could never forget him.

She knew that because he was so near, her heart was beating suffocatingly in her breast and she was conscious of the weakness he always evoked in her. At the same time, she had an inexpressible yearning to feel his lips once again on hers.

She thought for one wild moment that she might ask him to kiss her and then walk out of her life as he had walked into it.

But she knew that if he put his arms round her she would cling to him, her whole body would respond to his, and that wonderful magic would occur between them which would override all the wisdom and sense of her brain.

"I want you! I want you!" she longed to say.

Then she knew that he would never understand how desperately he disturbed her; how every nerve in her whole body was tense because of him.

Suddenly she gave a little cry.

"I must go back! It is getting late! If they find I am not in the house when they return they will begin to ask questions."

Lord Sheldon drew his gold watch from his pocket and glanced at it.

As if it told him that there was no time for argument, he said quietly:

"I will take you home."

"You cannot do that . . ." Azalea began.

"I will drop you near Flagstaff House, and you can walk up the drive. I think it unlikely that your Aunt has left the Governor's party so early, but one never knows!"

"I must change," Azalea cried.

She hurried away through the garden, glad that her feet had not been bound like Mrs. Chang's because she could move quickly when it was necessary.

Kai Yin Chang was waiting for her just inside the garden door.

"You have happy talk?" she asked.

"It is late!" Azalea replied. "I must change and hurry back. If my Aunt finds I have been out she will be very angry."

"She not know where you go," Mrs. Chang said comfortingly.

In the bed-room Azalea slipped out of her beautiful pink tunic and put on her tight corset and elaborate underclothes which seemed in contrast very hot and restricting.

"When you come again?" Kai Yin Chang asked.

"As soon as I can."

Then Azalea gave a little cry.

"What is it?" Mrs. Chang asked.

"I have just remembered that tomorrow my Uncle is taking my Aunt and the twins to luncheon in Renown Bay. They will start early and, as he has some troops to inspect over there, they will not be home until late."

"Good news!" Mrs. Chang exclaimed. "You come here."

She thought for a moment then added:

"Better idea! We go in Honourable husband's junk so you see Bay! Very beautiful! We visit islands."

"Could we do that?" Azalea asked.

She had already heard talk of the islands, how attractive they were, and she longed too to see the inside of a Chinese junk.

She had learnt that the rich merchants had special, elaborate junks which they used for cruising, rather like gentlemen in England using private yachts.

"You come here or go Quay?" Mrs. Chang enquired.

Azalea thought for a moment.

Either way was dangerous and she knew she would not be expected to leave Flagstaff House alone in a rickshaw without an escort.

If she said she was going shopping it might be more excusable than if she said she was going to the house of a Chinaman.

"I will meet you at the Quay."

"We look for you where big junks tied up."

By now Azalea was dressed in the pale-coloured cotton gown in which she had arrived.

She put on her hat, then she kissed Kai Yin Chang's soft cheek.

"Thank you. You are so kind."

"You very gracious," Mrs. Chang replied, and Azalea knew that she was touched at her show of affection.

Lord Sheldon was waiting near the front door.

Azalea thanked Mr. Chang and climbed into the carriage that was waiting.

The attendants wore the livery of Government

House and the horses were splendidly equipped, but Azalea was conscious of nothing but that Lord Sheldon was sitting beside her.

As the carriage started off he took her hand in his.

"I intend to see you again, Azalea," he said. "There is nothing you can say that will prevent me from doing so. It is best if you stop fighting me and let me cope with your Uncle and Aunt."

"No . . . please," Azalea pleaded, "please do not say . . . anything to . . . them."

He did not answer, but she saw his chin square a little and his lips tighten and knew with a sense of despair that he had no intention of listening to her pleadings.

"I will only consider doing what you ask," he said after a moment, "if you will tell me what this momentous secret is that makes you quite sure I am not even an acceptable acquaintance where you are concerned."

"I want to tell you," Azalea replied, "I want to do what you ask of me, but I cannot! It is impossible! There is really . . . nothing, therefore, we can . . . say to each other."

"Do you imagine I will accept that?" Lord Sheldon asked.

"But you must!" Azalea said. "And besides . . ."

Because she was feeling so positive her fingers had tightened on his, then suddenly what she was about to say died on her lips.

"There is no besides," Lord Sheldon interposed, "there is only us, Azalea—you and I. And you know as well as I do we have so much to learn about each other, so much to discover, and it cannot be done in the few snatched moments while we are watching the clock."

Even as he spoke the horses, which had been going downhill, were drawn to a standstill and Azalea recognised the outer wall of Flagstaff House. Fifty yards below them was the entrance to the drive.

As the footman began to get down from the box Lord Sheldon raised her hand to his lips.

"We shall meet again, Azalea," he said quietly. "Leave everything to me."

Because she had dressed in such a hurry Azalea had omitted to put on her gloves, and now she felt his lips warm and insistent against the softness of her skin.

She felt a little quiver of delight surge through her body, and then the footman opened the door of the carriage and she was obliged to step out.

There was so much she wanted to say to Lord Sheldon and yet she did not know what it was. She only knew that it was difficult to leave him.

She still wanted to plead with him to go away; and yet she wanted him to stay.

He did not alight with her but merely raised his hat, and as the footman clambered up onto the box the carriage moved off.

Azalea watched it until it was out of sight.

As she started to walk down the incline towards the gate of Flagstaff House, she knew that she loved him.

Azalea awoke the following morning with a feeling of irresistible excitement.

She had not been mistaken in thinking that her Aunt and the twins would be leaving early with the General.

Breakfast had been ordered at seven-thirty and before nine o'clock they had driven away from the house, escorted by four soldiers on horseback and with another carriage following them containing two Staff Officers and the Aides-de-Camp.

Lady Osmund had in fact returned from the Governor's garden-party in good humour.

Violet and Daisy had been a success not only with the socialites of Hong Kong but also with the Officers of the Regiments stationed there.

They had found their fresh, pink-and-white prettiness extremely attractive and in any case a new face was always an excitement for Regiments stationed abroad.

Lady Osmund had also been delighted with the manner in which Sir John Pope-Hennessey had singled her out and paid her special attention.

"Whatever you may say, Frederick," she said at dinner, "he is very charming."

"He can be pleasant," the General agreed. "At the same time, as I have told you before, Emily, he quarrels with everyone in authority. There is not a permanent Civil Servant in the place who has a good word to say for him, and my staff have been telling me of his quite outrageous behaviour to General Donovan."

The General paused and added harshly:

"I do not intend to be treated in such a fashion!"

"I am sure Sir John respects and admires you, Frederick," Lady Osmund said.

"One of the Colonial Office officials told me Sir John was sent a list of thirty-nine dispatches he never answered," the General continued. "He also stated that Sir John has muddled the finances of every Colony he has governed."

"Well, I beg of you not to quarrel with him, Frederick," Lady Osmund said firmly. "Hong Kong is really too small a place to contain opposing camps, and quite frankly I enjoy going to Government House. We are both dining there the day after tomorrow."

"I am quite happy to leave the social side to you, Emily," the General answered, "but I have no intention of giving in to the Governor, however objectionable he may make himself, where it concerns a matter of law and order."

"I am sure you will deal with that most competently," Lady Osmund said in a conciliatory tone.

But Azalea realised that she was not really interested.

"We had a lovely time, Azalea," Daisy told her when they were out of ear-shot of her mother, "and the Officers said such flatterings things to us it made Violet and me laugh!"

"There is a Ball on Friday night," Violet said, "and we are going to dance in the open air—fancy that!"

She paused and then because she was a kindly girl she added:

"I think it is very unkind of Mama not to let you

come, Azalea. I cannot think why she makes you stay at home."

"She has her reasons," Azalea replied, but she could not help feeling that it would be very wonderful to dance in the open air with Lord Sheldon.

She was sure he would dance well. At any rate, they would move in unison because they were so close in other ways.

In the darkness of the night she admitted to herself that she had loved him ever since he had first kissed her.

It would have been impossible that any man should evoke such wonderful and rapturous feelings without her loving him.

Since she had been starved of kindness and affection for the last two years, since she had come to England, it had been even more marvellous to know that he had even noticed her.

"I love him! I love him!" she whispered into her pillow and felt again the strange magic of his lips on hers.

She had tried not to think of how she had melted into his arms when they met in the Second Class of the *Orissa.*

She had been ashamed of herself for not having resisted him, or at least having tried to evade him, but she had known that he drew her to him with an inescapable magnetism that was something deeper and more fundamental than her own will.

"We belong to each other!" Azalea told herself.

Then she knew despairingly that it was only a question of time before he would return to England and she would never see him again.

He might want to see her. He might think he could arrange it, but her Uncle was far too apprehensive of what she might reveal about her father's death for him to tolerate even an acquaintanceship, let alone a friendship.

Now she thought how foolish she had been not to have taken the opportunities open to her during the long voyage on the *Orissa* to be with Lord Sheldon.

And yet she knew that instinctively she had been trying to save herself from suffering.

She thought now that it was inevitable since that moment in the Study that she should love him and that her love could only bring her the agony of parting and the inexpressible pain of saying good-bye.

She had tried to save herself and failed, and now she was hopelessly, helplessly in love. Her whole being cried out for him in a manner that in some ways was frightening.

Azalea knew that there was much of her mother's emotionalism in her; the deep Russian feelings that could never be understood by the controlled English, who were not, she thought, motivated by a fire.

That, she knew, was what burnt in her own veins when she thought of Lord Sheldon; a fire which surged like quick-silver through her blood and made her yearn for him with an intensity that made her blush.

"I love him!" she told herself, and knew that if he ordered her to walk bare-foot with him to India she would obey.

But always, standing over her like an avenging angel with a flaming sword, was the memory of her father's death and the disgrace that would be brought upon the family and the Regiment if it was ever known.

She was well aware that the British aristocracy were intensely proud of their families and their antecedents, and that Lord Sheldon's own history was one of honour and integrity.

Azalea was quite certain that if there was anything scandalous known about him in the past, any unsavoury gossip, her Aunt would have heard of it.

She guessed that even the General had a grudging admiration for him, even though he might deprecate his modern outlook and sympathy with the Governor's reforms.

Azalea's mind shied away from even saying to herself the word "marriage," but it was obvious that if by some miracle Lord Sheldon did love her he could never ask her to be his wife.

So what was the point, she asked herself, of inviting

unhappiness, of growing to love him more and more, knowing that it could never come to anything real and they could never be close to each other?

Despairingly she told herself that they were just ships that passed in the night.

She was a woman who had attracted him momentarily, first because she had surprised him by eavesdropping and perhaps he had wanted to punish her for her behaviour, and secondly because there was little competition on board the *Orissa*.

The other women were not very attractive and the majority of them were accompanied by their husbands.

She had intrigued him and therefore attracted his attention as she might not have done in any other circumstance.

It sounded a very plausible explanation—yet she knew there was a great deal more to it than that.

There was something between them; something that could never be explained away, however many words she expended on it.

As soon as her Aunt and Uncle had left, Azalea carried up to her bedroom a note-book in which she had written down a large number of instructions.

The majority were things that could quite easily be done tomorrow or the day after. There was no urgency about them and she knew that her Aunt had only thought of them in order to keep her fully occupied during their absence.

For once she was prepared to disobey orders.

Picking up her hat and putting a light shawl over her arm, she ran downstairs into the Hall.

She was glad to see that Ah Yok was there and she asked him for a rickshaw.

"You wish I come with you, Miss?" he asked in Cantonese.

Without having to explain to him that they must talk only English when her Aunt and Uncle were present, Ah Yok had known instinctively what she desired and spoke only Cantonese when there was no-one within hearing.

"I am going to the shops on the Quay," Azalea said.

"Tell the rickshaw-boy where to go and say that I will pay him off. I will find another rickshaw when it is time for me to return."

"Very good, Miss."

If Ah Yok was surprised at Azalea's independence, he was not in a position to say so.

He merely did what was asked of him and a few minutes later Azalea was trundling down the hill, and the rickshaw-boy was showing how good he was by travelling as fast as his legs could carry him.

They passed the cricket ground, the impressive Hong Kong Club, and went down Old Praya towards the part of the Quay where the junks were moored.

Azalea had to direct the boy a little further than Ah Yok had told him to go, but finally she saw several very large junks and told him to stop.

She paid him and even as she did so a servant was bowing at her side.

"Honourable guest of Mr. Chang?" he asked in his lilting voice.

Azalea nodded and he led her a little distance to where moored at the Quayside was the largest and most impressive-looking junk of them all.

It was painted red, its carvings were picked out in gold, and its bat-like sails were already being unfurled as Azalea stepped aboard to find Kai Yin waiting for her.

"You come! You come!" she exclaimed with delight. "I so afraid someone stop you."

"No, I am here," Azalea answered, looking round with delight, but Kai Yin, taking her by the hand, drew her down inside the junk.

There was a large Saloon furnished with comfortable couches, silk cushions, and embroidered stools.

"Honourable husband suggest," Kai Yin said, "wisest you wear Chinese clothes."

For a moment Azalea looked surprised and then she understood.

"You think if people see me they will wonder why I am on a junk?" she asked.

"English ladies not sail with Chinese," Kai Yin explained unnecessarily.

"Yes, of course. I never thought of that," Azalea smiled.

"I bring clothes so you look like me," Kai Yin told her.

She moved on her tiny feet to where Azalea could see a bed-room opening off the Saloon.

As in his house, Mr. Chang's taste was impeccable: the soft yellow of the panelled walls, the painted furniture with its carved corners, and the scroll-like pictures hanging on the walls were unlike the furnishings of any other ship.

Quickly Azalea took off her clothes and put on the comfortable tunic which Kai Yin had brought her.

This time it was of peony-red embroidered with bunches of apple-blossom, lined and piped with pink of the same shade, while the buttons at the neck and under the arms were of pink quartz.

The trousers were also pink, turned up with peony-red, and Kai Yin had brought Azalea not only hairpins with tops of pink quartz but also ear-rings and a bracelet to match them.

"How pretty!" Azalea exclaimed, and then admired Kai Yin's tunic of jade-green embroidered in shades of yellow and orange.

When she had arranged her hair Kai Yin picked up a little brush from her dressing-table and a cake of the black kohl with which she outlined her own eyes.

She applied it to Azalea's and very gently turned up the corners.

"Now you look Chinese," she said.

It did in fact, Azalea thought, make all the difference to her appearance.

She looked mysterious and enigmatic, and she could not help wondering if in Lord Sheldon's eyes she would appear even more secretive than usual.

"Honourable Aunt not know you!" Kai Yin cried gleefully, and Azalea was smiling when they went up on deck to find the junk moving out of the harbour.

They passed several English gun-boats and even a battle-ship, and although the sailors were leaning over the side to watch them go by she was quite certain that none of them guessed that she was of the same nationality as themselves.

But what delighted her more than the English vessels, the stately junks, and the clumsy dhows, were the sampans with their families.

She saw women leaning over the sides to do their washing; one was seated in the prow, feeding her baby, and another was plucking a chicken. There was a large coop of them attached to the side of the sampan.

It was all so fascinating and Kai Yin made her speak Chinese as she asked questions or pointed out things that amused or interested her.

Soon Azalea could look back and see Hong Kong Harbour behind them and Kowloon on their left.

There was a good breeze and now the sails were fully out and they were running before the wind.

Far in the distance were the high mountains of China, some of them peaking up into the clouds. The sun was very hot and soon Azalea was glad of the shade of the awnings which were erected for them on deck.

When Mr. Chang, who had been standing on the bridge directing the junk out of the harbour, came to join them, Azalea at last had the opportunity to ask him about his treasures.

He told her about the "Celestial horses," and the figures of tomb guardians he had collected, the winged cups of the Han period in lacquered wood, and the ceramic images of the Buddhist Deities he possessed.

He also explained to Azalea some of the legends and stories of the Gods.

Tien How was the Queen of Heaven. When she was born a strange light appeared in the sky and her room was filled with fragrance. After her death at an early age, the Sung Emperor had a narrow escape from a storm in the Yellow Sea. It was found that his ship was the only one carrying an image of the Goddess.

There was also Kuan Yin, the Goddess of Mercy, to whom every Chinese prayed at some time.

Kuan Yin was the kind and gentle Goddess to whom women brought their pleas for a male child and who loved the white and palest pink lotus flowers which were also, Azalea learnt, the favourite blossoms of Buddha.

Mr. Chang managed to make what he told her not only interesting but also exciting and stimulating to the mind.

Everything Chinese, Azalea began to realise, had a history that came from their past, and each had a special, esoteric meaning for those who searched for it.

She could understand that the poor Chinese, living in sampans with no other possessions except what floated with them, felt the need for help and succour from the Gods who they believed lived on the heights of the great mountains within sight, but out of reach.

Azalea said this to Mr. Chang and he replied:

"You are right! The Chinese believe that Kuan Yin looks down on them from the mountain-peaks and hears the cries of the world."

They sailed on for what seemed to Azalea a long way, and at noon they ate a delicious meal which was her first taste of genuine Chinese food.

On a round table prepared by the servants there were chopsticks and several little saucers containing oysters, soya beans, tomato sauce, and vinegar.

Hot, damp cloths moistened with rose-water were presented on a tray and Azalea lifted hers with the pair of silver tongs provided.

The meal began with a tiny, handleless cup of jasmine-scented Chinese tea. After this there were small cockles dipped in sauce, slices of abalone or haliotis shells, pieces of ginger, prawns, and stuffed olives.

Next came ducks and chickens cooked with lotus seeds, chestnuts, and walnuts; meat-balls wrapped in dough as light as thistledown; fledgling birds with tiny mushrooms; and a suckling pig, little bigger than a baby rabbit, with its crackling as fine as glass.

Azalea was beginning to feel she could eat no more, but Kai Yin told her the soup was "shark's-fin" and a great "speciality."

"At big party," she told Azalea in Chinese, "after soup you toast your host, saying, 'Yam Seng.' "

Blushing a little, Azalea raised her soup cup to Mr. Chang and, bowing, said:

"Yam Seng!"

"I thank you, Honourable Heung-Far," Mr. Chang replied.

Azalea looked surprised and Kai Yin explained that it was Cantonese for "Fragrant Flower."

A fish-dish followed—a whole carp covered in sweet-sour sauce—and after that came several sweet-meats. Then thin slices of orange in syrup were dipped in iced water to become a fine toffee.

To drink there was a sweet, warm wine distilled from rice and drunk from small porcelain cups.

It was all new and unusual to Azalea, and the only trouble was that when the meal ended she knew she had eaten too much!

While they ate, Azalea learnt that there were a great number of other Gods and Goddesses whom the Chinese worshipped.

There was Pei Ti, Supreme God of Profound Heaven, and Tam Kung, who had powers over the weather which he derived from the Nine Dragons of Kowloon.

"He provoke typhoon by throwing handfuls peas into air and put out fire with cup water," Kai Yin related, but her eyes were twinkling as she said it, and Azalea wondered if she really believed it was true.

"We have much feasting on Tam Kung's birthday," Mr. Chang continued, "feasting, sacrificing roast pigs, and lion-dancing, but the lucky thing to do to take joss-sticks from the Temple and bring them home still smouldering to place before household Gods."

Azalea had seen the little shrine in Kai Yin's apartments which was dedicated to the Gods, and she learnt that it was lucky for joss-sticks to be in threes and candles to be in twos.

"We believe it is very important," Mr. Chang told her, "to placate Tso Kwan, the Kitchen God. You will find him in almost every Chinese home and his shrine is usually in a niche near the stove represented by gold characters on a red tablet."

"If it is due to Tso Kwan that we have delicious food like this," Azalea smiled, "I am prepared to light any number of joss-sticks to him."

"He is supposed to be very fat and jovial as a result of too-good-living," Mr. Chang said, "but he is also of great importance because once every year he visits other Gods and reports on the behaviour of all the members of the household."

Azalea laughed.

"What an awful thought that he is making a list of all your failings and misdeeds!"

"It is very frightening," Mr. Chang agreed, "so before he sets out on New Year's Eve the family give him a feast when large quantities of honey are produced for him. This to try to seal his lips, or at least to make him utter only honeyed words."

"I do hope the honey is successful!" Azalea exclaimed.

"Crackers are fired to drive away the demons," Mr. Chang continued, "and on his return four days later he is welcomed with an abundance of good things. His tablet or picture is reinstated in the shrine with bowings and burning of incense."

After luncheon Mr. Chang went on deck. But because it had now become very hot, Azalea and Kai Yin rested on soft couches, talking until Azalea, because she was tired after having lain awake the night before, thinking of Lord Sheldon, fell asleep for a little while.

When she awoke it was to find that the junk was tied up to the jetty of an island.

"Can we go ashore?" she asked.

Kai Yin shook her head.

"No. Honourable husband say stay here while load cargo."

Azalea was surprised, but when she looked over the side she saw that a great number of large wooden chests were being carried along the very narrow wooden jetty by coolies who balanced them on their heads.

She was not sure, but she had an idea that the chests contained opium.

She had learnt that on the Praya in Hong Kong

large square packets weighing a hundredweight each
of Indian opium arrived in their thousands every week,
and were worth, when the crude drug had been
prepared, £140 a packet.

The opium trade, one of the Aides-de-Camp had
told her, was chiefly in the hands of Parsees, who wore
high, stiff black hats and held the monopoly for selling
and preparing opium.

Azalea longed to ask Mr. Chang if he was in fact
taking opium on board, but as he did not volunteer
what his cargo contained, she felt shy of appearing
curious.

It was soon loaded, and as the junk turned for home
Azalea knew with a sinking of her heart that her day
of delight was nearly over.

There was so much more she wanted to know, so
much she wanted to learn, and she hoped that Mr.
Chang would come to the cabin so that she would have
a chance to question him further.

In the meantime, she stood on deck watching the
small islands fade away into insignificance, and saw another view of the high Chinese mountains and watched
the sails of junks like great fluttering birds move across
the blue sea.

It was still very hot and after a little while Kai Yin
said she must go down to the Saloon and rather reluctantly Azalea followed her.

"We must go on deck as we near Hong Kong," she
said. "I want to see the harbour and the ships. It is
very romantic, with the great peak towering above the
town."

"I glad you like Hong Kong," Kai Yin said, "very
happy place. I glad I Hong Kong wife!"

Azalea was just going to say she thought she was a
very beautiful one when suddenly there was the noise
of gun-fire! It was followed by voices shouting, and
again the rattle of shots followed, by a piercing scream.

Azalea jumped to her feet.

"What is happening?" she asked, and would have run
across the cabin to the door if Kai Yin had not stopped
her by putting her arms round her.

"No! No!" she cried. "It dangerous!"

"But what is it? What is happening?" Azalea asked.

"Pirates!" Kai Yin replied.

She pulled Azalea down onto a couch and they sat there with their arms round each other, listening to the sounds overhead.

The gun-fire had ceased but there were raucous and offensive shouts which sounded like men giving orders, but there were no further screams.

They waited, trembling, for what seemed a long time.

Then the cabin door burst open and Azalea saw what she knew at first glance must indeed be pirates.

They were dressed roughly in conventional Chinese garb but round their waists they wore wide leather belts into which were stuck pistols and knives.

They had a rough, ferocious look which was very frightening.

The leading pirate, and there were about half a dozen of them behind him, stared at Azalea and Kai Yin as if in surprise.

Then he gave an order over his shoulder to the men who were following him. Two of them walked through the Saloon to fling open the door of the bed-room.

Azalea followed them with her eyes and she therefore gave a cry of surprise and terror as another man picked her up in his arms.

Kai Yin was also lifted from the couch and as Azalea tried to struggle he threw her over his shoulder and, with her head hanging down his back, climbed up the companion-way and onto the deck.

There she saw a scene of utter confusion.

One of the masts had been torn down and the sail had fallen partly over the bridge.

A man was lying on deck with a crimson spot on his chest and she thought he must be dead.

Other sailors were having their hands tied behind their backs but as far as Azalea could see there was no sign of Mr. Chang.

It was difficult to take in everything as she hung

head-downward while her feet and body were held tightly by the man who carried her.

She saw that Kai Yin was following, which in itself was a comfort as she was carried over the side of the junk and onto another, smaller ship that was lying alongside it.

She had a quick glimpse of the deck on which articles removed from the junk were being piled, which included the chests which they had taken aboard at the island and other objects such as pails, brushes, cooking utensils, and a number of unidentifiable objects which were laid round the centre mast.

Then Azalea was carried down a narrow companion-way and into a very small, dirty cabin which seemed almost dark.

She was flung roughly onto a pile of sacking, and before she had time to recover her breath, Kai Yin was thrown down beside her.

The men looked at them both and it seemed to Azalea that their faces were quite expressionless. Then they left the cabin, closing the door behind them, and Azalea heard a bolt shoot into place.

She turned despairingly to Kai Yin.

"What is happening? Where will they take us?" she asked.

Kai Yin put her hands up to her face and Azalea knew that she was crying.

"They kill Honourable husband," she wept. "I not see him. I sure he dead!"

Azalea put her arms round her.

"You cannot be sure of that," she said comfortingly.

"And we be sold!" Kai Yin cried.

"Sold?" Azalea ejaculated. "What do you mean?"

She remembered as she spoke the conversation her Uncle had had at luncheon about the women who were kidnapped and sold either as household slaves or—frighteningly—for immoral purposes.

'It cannot be true!' she thought.

It must be a nightmare that this should happen, and yet she knew there was nothing either Kai Yin or she could do about it.

Chapter Six

For a moment Azalea felt as if her brain were filled with wool and she could not think.

She only knew that her breath seemed still to be knocked out of her as it had been when she was thrown down on the sacking.

Then she realised that Kai Yin was sobbing uncontrollably and she knew she must somehow comfort her.

"Perhaps Mr. Chang is safe," she said. "They may not have killed him but only taken him prisoner."

"If prisoner, I see on deck," Kai Yin replied, and continued to cry against Azalea's shoulder.

"I thought the pirates were finished," Azalea said after a minute, almost as if she spoke to herself.

"Always pirates," Kai Yin muttered.

Azalea tried to remember what she had read about pirates in the book on Hong Kong she had found in the Library on the *Orissa*.

It was a history of the Colony and she had gathered quite a lot of facts from it.

One thing that had been described fully was the overwhelming damage done by pirates to trading vessels at the beginning of the British occupation. But Azalea was sure it was claimed that in recent years the Navy had dispersed the pirate fleets.

She had a good memory and now she concentrated on recalling how the peaceful trading junks in the early 1850s had to be heavily armed because the pirates were waiting for them as soon as they were clear of the harbour.

It was thought then that the pirate fleets made Hong Kong their headquarters and that native marine-store keepers not only supplied them with arms and ammunition but also helped them dispose of their booty.

There had been suspicion, she remembered, that well-paid spies in mercantile offices and Government departments gave them information concerning the shipments of valuable cargo and, even more important, the movements of the Police and the British gun-boats.

Now, frighteningly, Azalea recalled that there had been a battle between the Navy and sixty-four pirate junks manned by over three thousand men, in which the majority were destroyed.

There had even been an encounter in Aberdeen Bay, which was not far from Victoria, between piratical junks and eight Chinese gun-boats.

One case heard in the Hong Kong Courts in 1952 was particularly shocking because it concerned the murder of the Captain, the Officers, and the passengers of a British steamship.

"I am sure the book said things were better now," Azalea muttered to herself.

She remembered that in one battle the British Navy had burned twenty-three pirate junks and killed twelve hundred men at Sherifoo, with the loss of only one Commander and nineteen men wounded.

"Perhaps we are mistaken," she told herself, "and these pirates will not kill and murder as they did in the old days."

But she could not help recalling the shots, the man lying on the deck, the crimson stain of blood on his chest, and knew that, however optimistic she might try to be, there had undoubtedly been casualties when the junk was boarded.

Kai Yin went on crying and Azalea continued to try to remember all that had been said in the book she had read.

Unfortunately, she had been so interested in reading about the beauties of Hong Kong, the Chinese customs, and the development of the Colony that she had not been particularly interested in what was said about the pirates.

And yet she was almost certain in her mind that the position was said to have improved considerably under Governor Sir Richard Macdonnell.

He had established a combination of Harbour-Office and Police-Office duties, after which he had reported:

> *Not one single trial for piracy took place during the years 1869 and 1870.*

Yet however consoling this might be, Mr. Chang's junk had certainly been attacked and the cargo which had been loaded from the island had obviously been the attraction.

It was clear the pirates had not expected to find women aboard, but Kai Yin's fear that they would be sold was obviously a possibility and Azalea felt herself tremble at the thought.

How could they possibly escape? And more important, where were they being taken?

Azalea could feel the satin of her tunic being soaked with Kai Yin's tears but she was not crying as violently as she had at first.

"Try to be brave," Azalea pleaded. "And I want you to tell me all that you know about women being kidnapped. I would rather be prepared for what might happen than to be shocked when it does."

With what was clearly a tremendous effort, Kai Yin raised her head from Azalea's shoulder and wiped her eyes with a minute silk handkerchief which she took from the wide sleeves of her tunic.

Although she seemed a typically helpless and subservient Chinese woman, Kai Yin was quite intelligent.

It took Azalea a little time to understand what she was saying, especially as she was too agitated to speak in anything but Chinese.

Gradually she pieced together a picture of the kidnapping of women and girls which had raised an acute conflict between the British law and Chinese customs.

According to Kai Yin, the number of kidnappers

coming before the Courts was increasing every year, and kidnapping was becoming more popular because the girls were bought to be sent overseas where the price of sale might be as high as £350.00.

"In Hong Kong price only forty-five pounds," she said scornfully.

Because the trading was advantageous, women were lured into Hong Kong on completely false promises.

But, as the General had said, attempts to stop the kidnapping brought the authorities up against the deeply rooted Chinese custom of the purchase of children for adoption and particularly of girls as domestic servants.

This practice was called *Mui Tsai.*

The situation so worried the authorities that Kai Yin had heard from her husband that the English and Chinese together were considering setting up an anti-kidnapping society.

This in fact would become the Society for the Protection of Virtue, or in Chinese words *Po Leung Kuk.*

"Honourable husband think good idea," Kai Yin said. "He support British, tell Governor he give money."

Azalea longed to say that she wished the Society had started already, but she was well aware that she must not show her fear too obviously or Kai Yin would start to cry again.

"Do you think it would be wise for me to tell the pirates that I am English?" Azalea asked.

Kai Yin gave a scream of protest.

"No, no! Very dangerous!" she exclaimed. "Some pirates spare Chinese but kill British. You pretend be Chinese."

It certainly made sense, Azalea thought, but she wondered how long she could keep up the deception, seeing that her Chinese was halting and she very often used the wrong words.

"I talk," Kai Yin said, "you say nothing."

It seemed, however, at the moment there was no chance of either of them saying anything.

The ship in which they were imprisoned was now

moving, and the reason the cabin had been dark, Azalea realised, was that the one small port-hole in their prison had been against the side of the junk.

Seeing that the sunshine was now coming in through the dirty, salt-stained glass, Azalea rose to look out and when she did so gave an exclamation of horror.

"What matter? What wrong?" Kai Yin cried. "What you see?"

For a moment Azalea did not answer, then she decided not to tell Kai Yin the truth!

They were already perhaps fifty yards from Mr. Chang's junk and the pirates had set it on fire!

She could see the flames licking at the base of the sails and there was thick black smoke coming from the Saloon.

She remembered now that she had heard that the pirates would strip their prey and then burn it so that there would be no evidence against them.

The wanton destruction of ships seemed to her terrible, especially of a junk as beautiful and expensive as Mr. Chang's. But even more important was the anxiety as to whether anyone had been left on board alive.

There was no sign of any movement, and yet Azalea could not help wondering what the pirates had done with the sailors whose hands they had tied behind their backs.

It would have been easy, she thought, to murder them by throwing them overboard, knowing they would be unable to swim; or perhaps they had been placed below decks where they would burn to death.

"What you see?" Kai Yin asked again, and Azalea turned towards her to say quietly:

"Nothing. I was only upset because we are sailing in the opposite direction to Hong Kong."

There was nothing either of them could do, she thought to herself, and what was the point of upsetting Kai Yin, who, even if her husband was dead, as she feared, would not wish his body to be burned at sea.

She sat down once again on a pile of sacking to say:

"We must be very brave. There is nothing to be

gained by making scenes or antagonising our captors. Where do you think they will take us?"

Kai Yin shrugged her shoulders.

"Many places. All give big money superior Chinese girls."

"They will know I am not superior when they see my feet," Azalea said.

"Then you be servant," Kai Yin replied.

Azalea thought this might in fact be preferable to the other fate which might await her, but she was not certain.

She only knew that she was frightened, desperately frightened, of what the future might hold, but there was no point in expressing her feelings.

She could only pray in her heart that it might not be as bad as she anticipated.

Now that the ship was at sea there was a great deal of bumping and banging and it sounded as if the crates that had been taken from the junk were being carried below and stacked outside their cabin.

But there were no longer loud voices or harsh orders, and perhaps, Azalea thought, the silence, except for the noise of the crates being handled, was even more frightening than if the men had sworn or shouted at one another.

She heard their feet padding above them, a sound very different from that made by European sailors, and now that the ship was moving there was the creak the masts made, the slap of the sails, and the beating of the waves against the wooden sides.

Kai Yin had been silent for some minutes, then suddenly she said in a quiet, firm voice:

"No man touch wife of Honourable husband—I die!"

Azalea looked at her in consternation.

"You must not do that!"

"I kill myself!" Kai Yin said firmly. "Much worse be defamed, insulted, then lose face!"

"It is not a question of losing face," Azalea said, knowing how much this meant to the Chinese. "It would mean that you had given up hope of being rescued, and in England we say: 'While there is life there is hope.' "

"No hope," Kai Yin said firmly. "I wife of Honourable man—Mr. Chang wish me die."

"You cannot be sure of that," Azalea protested.

As she spoke she realised how much the humiliation of losing face meant.

She had heard so many stories of men who would starve rather than take a job which they thought would degrade them; of Chinese who had cut their throats because of some quite minor dispute in which they had been the loser.

She had always thought these were tales invented about the Chinese because they were an enigmatic race.

Now she was not sure.

There was a dignity about Kai Yin that had not been noticeable before, but it was always difficult to interpret her emotions because her face could be so impassive.

She sat with her back very straight and her eyes were narrow slits.

"Please, Kai Yin," Azalea begged, "do not think of anything so horrible. Besides, you cannot leave me! I should be so frightened without you!"

"We separated when sold," Kai Yin answered. "Where I go there be knife. Easy die by knife."

"No, no!" Azalea pleaded. "You cannot talk like that. It is wrong—and very wicked to take one's own life."

"Chinese Gods not angry," Kai Yin replied. "They understand."

Azalea used every possible argument she could think of, but she knew it was to no avail.

It seemed to her as if Kai Yin had grown up suddenly. From being the soft, sweet, pampered young wife of an older man she had suddenly become a woman with principles, with an ideal of honour from which she would not be diverted.

Despairingly Azalea knew that if Kai Yin said she would kill herself, then that was what she would do.

Life was always cheap to the Chinese, and especially so where women were concerned. Girl babies were lucky to survive.

There were even places, Azalea had heard, on the outskirts of towns in China where there were notices saying: "Girls must not be drowned here."

Too many girls in a family was a financial disaster, and to avoid this the baby was left out in the sun to die or, more mercifully, smothered and buried hastily so that no-one would notice the shame of having another daughter.

It seemed a horrifying thought that Kai Yin, who had lived only for seventeen years, should die by her own hand. Yet Azalea could not help wondering as she thought of what lay ahead whether it was not in fact the wiser course.

Would she be able to stand the terror of being sold to a Chinese master who could treat her as a slave? Or, worse still, forced into a immoral life, the details of which she did not entirely understand?

Azalea was innocent, as were all English girls of her age. At the same time, she had read a great deal and lived in foreign countries.

She was aware of what Colonel Stewart, whom her father had killed, had intended to do with the daughter of their *dhirzi* after he had beaten her.

It was not just the first or second time this had happened, and the whispers about his behaviour had been heard by Azalea even though her mother had tried to protect her from the knowledge of such evil.

And because she talked with the Indian servants she had known that to them love was a beautiful thing, a gift from the Gods.

They worshipped the act of fertility; she had known what the phallic symbols on the Temples meant and the little shrines of the lingam by the wayside at which peasant-women left pathetic little offerings of flowers and rice.

Because she had spent most of her life in India, the beauty and the wonder of Krishna, the God of Love, was to her all that love could mean when a man and a woman belonged to each other and became one.

The Indians were intrinsically moral: their women were kept in purdah and the purity of Indian married life was unassailable.

That was what Azalea herself had hoped to find one day in marriage.

What lay ahead of her now, if Kai Yin was to be believed, was not marriage with purity, but something foul and so degrading that she could not even imagine the depths of humiliation to which it would subject her.

"Kai Yin is right," she told herself. "I too must die!"

Every nerve in her body shrank from the thought! Then she knew that if any man even kissed her after she had been kissed by Lord Sheldon, she would feel unclean.

She had loved him from the first moment he had taken her in his arms by surprise, when she had been unable to move, unable to struggle or run away.

It was love when one belonged instinctively not only in mind and body but also in spirit to a man. Love was the indefinable magic which drew two people together as if they had been part of each other in a past existence and were spiritually indivisible.

"I have belonged to him before," Azalea told herself now, "and therefore I can never belong to any other man."

She and Kai Yin sat silent on the dirty sacking and they were both in their own ways thinking how they must die.

"Supposing I only wounded myself?" Azalea questioned.

Then she thought it would be stupid to try to kill herself by the same method that Kai Yin would use.

The Chinese were experts at suicide.

Kai Yin would know the right place in the body in which to insert a knife so that death would be instantaneous, but for Azalea there was a better way.

When they took her up on deck she would throw herself into the sea and hope that she would not be rescued.

Most Chinese could not swim, and it was a tradition amongst seamen of all Nations that if their ship foundered it was best to drown quickly and not prolong the agony by trying to keep afloat.

'I will throw myself over the side of the ship!' Azalea thought. 'By the time the pirates realise what has happened I shall have drowned!'

She could not swim. Her Uncle would have been horrified at the thought of either the twins or herself being seen undressed in public.

In India it had not been safe to bathe in the great water-tanks which stood outside every village.

"I shall die quickly!" Azalea told herself, and tried to be consoled by the thought that although she would never see Lord Sheldon again he would remember her as he had seen her yesterday.

"You are beautiful!" he had said in the garden, and she could feel again the quiver that had gone through her at his words.

"Can you really believe," he had said later, "That we can walk away from each other and forget what our lips have said not in words but with a kiss?"

She would never forget as long as she lived, and perhaps he would remember her sometimes in the future; when he stood in another garden as beautiful as Mr. Chang's, or when he saw a Blue Magpie wing its way into the sunshine.

"Let us hope they bring us luck!" he had said.

But there was now no luck, Azalea thought, where she was concerned. There was only death, with the green waves closing over her head as she sank to the bottom of the ocean.

Because she could hardly bear her own thoughts, she rose restlessly to walk once again across the cabin to the port-hole.

She hoped to have a last sight of the junk even though it was in flames, but now the pirate ship had tacked from side to side to get the wind and there was nothing to be seen except in the distance the outline of an island.

It was green and mountainous but Azalea had no idea where it was.

They might, she thought, be swinging back on their tracks and going towards China, or again it might be to one of the many islands they must pass before they reached the ocean.

Kai Yin did not speak and Azalea thought that she was perhaps praying to Kuan Yin, the Goddess of Mercy.

"Oh, God, send us help," Azalea prayed. "Even now you could save us from what lies . . . ahead."

She felt as if her prayer was weak and ineffective. Then she remembered that her mother had always told her that prayers from the heart were always heard.

They had been visiting a Temple in India and Azalea, who was very young at the time, had watched the women in their colourful saris praying at the shrine of the Elephant God.

"How can they think that funny God with the Elephant's head can hear them, Mama?" she had asked.

"It is the prayer that matters, Azalea," her mother answered. "When a prayer comes from the heart, there is always Someone who will listen; Someone too big and too wonderful for us to understand. But He is there! Although He may appear in different forms to different people, God is there for everyone."

Azalea had been too young to comprehend exactly what her mother had meant at the time.

But afterwards, when she had grown to understand a little of the Indian religions and realised the sacrifices the Hindus, the Moslems, and the Buddhists made for the Gods they worshipped, she began to understand.

Now she was sure that Kuan Yin, the Goddess of Mercy to whom Kai Yin was praying, and the God to whom she herself prayed were one.

"Please . . . please help us," she prayed again, and imagined her prayer being carried like the wings of a blue bird up into the sky above them.

There was a sudden explosion so loud that the whole ship seemed to vibrate with it.

Azalea gave a little scream and clasped her arms

round Kai Yin as if to protect her. The Chinese girl clung to her.

"What . . . happens?" she asked in a frightened whisper.

Any answer Azalea might have made was drowned by the noise of a gun being fired from the deck above them, and this time the sound was deafening.

Again there was an explosion and Azalea knew that it was made by a big gun which was attacking them.

The shell had not hit the ship but had exploded in the water beside it. She heard the splash of the heavy spray on the deck and then the water washing overboard, so that it slid down over the port-hole.

Releasing Kai Yin, Azalea ran across the cabin.

She looked out and gave a shrill cry.

"It is a ship! A British ship!"

For a moment Kai Yin looked at her as if she could not take in what she had said.

"I can see the White Ensign!" Azalea cried. "We are safe! Kai Yin . . . we are safe!"

"They kill us!" Kai Yin said. "They kill us before British sailors come on board!"

There was a note of terror in her voice which told Azalea that she believed what she was saying.

It was in fact quite likely, she thought. The pirates would be tried for piracy, but if there was also a charge of kidnapping their sentence would be harsher.

Even as she thought it, she heard feet coming down the companion-way and rushed to the cabin door.

There was a bolt on the inside although not a very adequate one, just a flat piece of wood which slotted into a wooden lock fixed on the wall.

She jammed it home.

She had only just done so when she heard the bolt on the other side being dragged back and the door was shaken as someone tried to open it.

Azalea put out both her hands and pressed herself against it.

She realised that she had little strength compared with the man who was trying to reach them. At the same time, combined with the bolt, she might be able to hold the door closed until the ship was boarded.

The sound up above grew deafening. After a short exchange of rifle-shots she could hear orders being given in Cantonese, but by a very English-sounding voice.

The man on the other side of the door was shaking it furiously.

Azalea fancied that he put his shoulder to it but, although the bolt creaked, it held. Then suddenly she heard him run away, his feet padding over the boards.

There was the sound of heavy footsteps descending the companion-way, and a very English voice said:

"Here is the cargo! Opium, as I expected!"

Azalea felt herself sagging against the door.

Even after the assailant on the other side had gone, she still pressed with all her strength against the bare wood, terrified that at the last second the bolt would give and he would burst in upon them.

She was quite certain that he would have carried in his hand one of the long, carved knives that all the pirates wore in their belts.

Kai Yin had not stirred.

She was still sitting motionless on the sacking, looking like a flower in her coloured tunic, and her face was very pale, as if she could not realise or understand that they were safe and was still preparing herself for the moment when she must die.

"You had better get this stuff out of here," Azalea heard a man say outside. "And see if there is anyone in those cabins."

With a hand that shook, Azalea pulled back the bolt and opened the door.

Outside stood an Officer in white uniform, looking at the great pile of chests which had been taken from Mr. Chang's junk.

Beside him stood several Naval ratings in their white jumpers and blue trousers, their round, white-topped caps on their heads.

They all turned to look at Azalea and as they did so someone came down the companion-way.

As he reached the bottom Azalea turned her head.

For a moment it was impossible to move.

"Azalea!" he exclaimed.

She ran towards him and felt his arms go round her. It was like reaching Heaven. Her prayers had been answered and she was safe.

As *HMS Fury* carried them back to Hong Kong, Azalea, sitting in a cabin with Lord Sheldon, learnt what had happened.

Next door Kai Yin was sitting beside a bunk on which Mr. Chang lay with his arm bandaged.

It hardly seemed possible that he should be alive after Azalea had seen the junk burning and had known that the pirates had set it on fire, having looted everything they considered valuable.

"It was the burning junk we saw first," Lord Sheldon told her. "One of the sailors drew our attention to it and Captain Marriott was immediately suspicious that it might be the work of pirates.

" 'They loot and burn,' he told me, 'and unless we are lucky enough to see the junk in flames, there is no evidence to connect it with them once they have the cargo in their own ship.'

"We steamed towards the burning junk," Lord Sheldon continued, "and as we drew nearer to it Captain Marriott said:

" 'I believe that is Mr. Chang's junk. I have always admired it. I think it is one of the most attractive in the whole of Victoria Harbour!' "

Lord Sheldon's arm tightened round Azalea as he said:

"It was then that I became afraid."

"You thought I might be on board?"

"You do such unpredictable things that nothing surprises me!" he replied. "And I had the feeling that sooner or later you would find it impossible to resist sailing in the harbour and seeing the beauty of the islands."

"Why were you on this cruiser?" Azalea enquired.

"I arranged several days ago to inspect some of the

British fighting vessels. Captain Marriott was deputed by the Governor to escort me. We had luncheon on the battle-ship, visited two gun-boats, and were just returning to the harbour. Thank God I found you in time!"

Azalea turned her face against his shoulder.

"Kai Yin thought that as the pirates had kidnapped us they would . . . sell us," she whispered.

"You must forget what might have happened," Lord Sheldon said quietly. "It is something which could occur only once in a lifetime. Piracy has been put down so successfully by the Navy in the last few years that they were saying at luncheon there is really very little for the gun-boats to do these days."

"The pirates were very . . . frightening."

"They are deliberately aggressive," Lord Sheldon explained. "It makes the Chinese willing without argument to do anything that is demanded of them."

"But they shot at the sailors on Mr. Chang's junk."

"They killed one man and they will be punished."

"Why did they wound Mr. Chang?"

"He resisted them, so they fired at him. As it happened, the bullet only wounded him in the shoulder. Then he was clever enough to realise that the best thing he could do was to pretend to be dead. He fell down on the deck and closed his eyes. After that they paid no further attention to him!"

"Thank goodness!" Azalea exclaimed, thinking how unhappy Kai Yin had been.

"When the pirates had left, Mr. Chang tried to put out the flames with his uninjured arm," Lord Sheldon went on.

"That was brave!"

"Very brave! And it was very fortunate that he was alive, because otherwise we might not have been in such a hurry to follow the pirates and save both you and Mrs. Chang."

"What happened to the rest of the crew?" Azalea asked.

"We found them tied up on the deck of the pirate ship. Most of them, I imagine, to save themselves would have joined the pirates, who are always looking

for able seamen. Those who refuse to do so seldom live
to tell the tale!"

Azalea gave a little shiver.

"It has been a terrible experience for you," Lord
Sheldon said, "but I want you to be sensible and deter-
mine to put it out of your mind. As I have said, it will
never happen to you again, and the pirate-gang will
undoubtedly pay the price for their crimes."

"Kidnapping will still go on," Azalea said.

"That is true," Lord Sheldon agreed, "but that is
something which the Governor is determined to stop,
and I shall support him in every possible way."

He smiled as he said gently:

"I have a very personal motive for fighting against it
now."

He looked down at Azalea as he spoke, then put his
fingers under her chin and turned her face up to his.

"You will never know what I went through when I
learnt you were a prisoner on a pirate-ship. They did
not actually hurt you?"

"No," Azalea answered. "They carried us down the
companion-way and locked us in the cabin."

She paused and said:

"It became really terrifying only at the last moment,
when Kai Yin thought they would kill us before you
came aboard. A man did try to open the door, but I
had bolted it on the inside."

"You were very brave, my darling," Lord Sheldon
said.

Then he bent his head and his lips were on Azalea's.

He kissed her passionately and in a manner that was
different from the kisses he had given her before.

She knew it was because he had been afraid for her,
and yet it was difficult to think because once again she
felt the ecstasy and wonder that his kisses had aroused
in her before.

But now his mouth was more demanding, more insistent, so that the fire within her awoke to meet the
fire in him.

"I love you! God, how I love you!" Lord Sheldon
exclaimed.

Then he was frantically kissing her forehead, her eyes, her cheeks, the softness of her neck above the high collar of her tunic, and then again her lips.

The fact that she was wearing Chinese dress and was not restricted by her boned corsets made her body very soft and yielding against his.

He held her closer and still closer to him until it seemed to Azalea, with their hearts beating against each other's, that they became one person.

"I love you!" he said again.

Looking down at her eyes, at the faint blush on her cheeks, and at the warm softness of her parted lips, he said gently:

"How soon will you marry me, my precious?"

As if by his words he had thrown a jug of cold water over her, Azalea felt herself stiffen. Then she moved a little way away from him, her hands pressing against him.

"Why not? You love me—I know you do!"

"What is it? What is the matter?" he asked.

"I cannot . . . marry . . . you!"

"I do love you," Azalea answered, "I love you with every part of me . . . my heart . . . my soul, and beyond my hope of Heaven . . . but I shall never be . . . allowed to be your . . . wife!"

"This is nonsense!" Lord Sheldon began, then stopped. "Are we back with your secrets? Can they possibly, whatever they may be, matter more than our love and the fact that you belong to me, you are mine?"

"They matter," Azalea answered, "because I cannot tell you what my secret is . . . and yet because of . . . it my Uncle will never . . . allow me to . . . marry you!"

"I will speak to the General myself!"

"It would be . . . useless!"

"Then if he will not give me his consent, I will marry you without it!" Lord Sheldon said firmly.

"He is my Guardian," Azalea replied.

They both knew that a Guardian could not only arrange a marriage but also prevent one.

A girl was completely and legally under the jurisdiction of her Guardian, just as she was under the direction of her parents.

What was more, there was no need to put into words that Azalea was under age. But even when she was twenty-one the General could still refuse any suitor without even consulting her.

Lord Sheldon was silent for a moment. Then he said:

"This is the first time in my life, Azalea, that I have ever asked a woman to marry me. I had no intention of getting married, and although I admit to having had a great many love-affairs in my life I have never really been in love."

He saw the expression in her eyes and for a moment laid his lips against hers.

It was a very light kiss, and yet it was the kiss of a man who knows that something is so precious, so perfect, that he cannot help acknowledging the wonder of it.

"I think the night I first kissed you," Lord Sheldon went on, "I knew that something perfect and unique had happened to me. I could not forget the feeling of your lips beneath mine, and I could not ignore the strange, unusual feelings that kiss aroused in us both."

He paused to say softly:

"I am not wrong in thinking that you felt as I did?"

"It was wonderful!" Azalea replied, "so wonderful that I could not prevent you from kissing me . . . even though I knew I should do so . . . and afterwards I could not believe it was true. It was a . . . magic I could not describe . . . even to myself."

"That is the right word for it," Lord Sheldon said. "It was magic, even though I told myself I must have been mistaken or perhaps the General's whisky was unusually strong!"

"And . . . when you saw me again . . ." Azalea asked.

"I knew that you were the woman I had been seeking all my life. I would not acknowledge at first, even to myself, that I intended to marry you. And yet now I think that my heart was sure that we belonged to each other even though my brain was still ready to be sceptical."

He gave a little laugh.

"You bemused and bewildered me, as you still do. You have yet to explain why you read your Uncle's secret file on Hong Kong. Why you speak Russian, and why you tried to avoid me on the ship and were extremely successful in doing so."

Once again he put his fingers under Azalea's chin and turning her face up to his said fiercely:

"How could you make us waste so much time aboard the *Orissa*, when I might have been holding you in my arms and kissing you?"

His lips were on hers as he spoke the last word, and she was conscious only of the rising desire within herself, of the glory and the fire that drew them so close to each other that it was hard to breathe.

"I want you!" Lord Sheldon said in his deep voice. "I want you now, at this moment and for all eternity. You are mine, Azalea! You belong to me!"

"I believe that too," Azalea murmured, "and I feel that we have ... belonged to each other in ... previous lives."

"I am sure of it," he answered. "I have lived in India long enough to know there is no other reasonable explanation for the strivings, the hunger, the unhappiness of mankind. My happiness lies with you!"

"And mine with ... you," Azalea whispered.

"So we come back to where we started," Lord Sheldon said with a little smile. "When will you marry me?"

"You do not understand," Azalea said miserably, "and there is ... nothing I can do to make you ... I can only tell you that I shall love you all my life and in the here-after ... but I shall never be ... allowed to be your ... wife."

"Damn the here-after!" Lord Sheldon exclaimed violently. "I am not interested in anything but the present! I want you, Azalea, and I intend to have you, and I promise you I do not give up easily."

She would have argued with him, but once again his lips were on hers.

He kissed her until it was impossible to think; impossible to be aware of anything but the raging, burning fire of his lips and the pulsating of her body.

He held her closer and closer, and it was only when they heard voices giving orders on deck that they realised they had reached the harbour.

With a sinking feeling in her heart Azalea remembered that she had to return to Flagstaff House.

Explanations would have to be made about where she had been and why she was dressed in Chinese clothes.

She drew herself away from Lord Sheldon's arms, and the problems and difficulties rushed into her mind like an invading force of pirates.

Because they were close to each other there was no need for her to put her thoughts into words.

"I will make all the explanations," he said gently. "All that matters is that you are safe, and that is what I shall make your Uncle understand."

Azalea shuddered.

"Perhaps ... they will not yet be ... back," she faltered, knowing even as she spoke that it was a forlorn hope.

The sun was sinking and although she did not know the time she felt it must be well after six o'clock. The General always aimed to return at the very latest by that hour.

"Leave everything to me!" Lord Sheldon said, then as if he could not help himself he kissed Azalea's forehead.

Anxious as she was to get back to Flagstaff House, Azalea knew that she could not hurry away until she was certain Mr. Chang was taken safely ashore.

Fortunately his own carriage was at the Quay, and he was carried to it on a stretcher, his wife following behind.

Azalea kissed Kai Yin good-bye.

"You come see me soon," she begged.

"As soon as I can," Azalea answered, "but you will be busy looking after Mr. Chang."

"Honourable husband live—all that matters!" Kai Yin said with tears in her eyes.

Azalea kissed her again.

Feeling somewhat self-conscious about her appearance, Azalea said good-bye to Captain Marriott and thanked him. Then with Lord Sheldon at her side she was driven off in a closed carriage towards Flagstaff House.

Apprehensive of what lay ahead, she slipped her hand into his and felt the warm strength of his fingers.

They were comforting and a source of courage.

"You are not to be afraid," he said. "You are just to trust me, Azalea. I promise you I always get my own way!"

"I want to believe you," she answered, "and you know I trust you."

"Then do not look so worried, my darling," he said. "You have the most beautiful eyes I have seen in my whole life, but I want to take that worried expression away from them. I want you to look happy, young and untroubled, and that is how I intend you to look, even if it takes a lifetime to achieve it."

Azalea laid her cheek for a moment against his shoulder.

"I am utterly happy when I am with you. I have been so miserable these past years since Papa died that, now that you love me, it is like coming out of a dark tunnel into the sunlight."

"How did your father die?" Lord Sheldon asked.

Azalea stiffened. She had never expected to be asked this question and she could not think of an answer.

Without meaning to her fingers tightened on Lord Sheldon's. Then as she realised he was waiting for a reply to his question, she stammered:

"T-typhoid . . . h-he died of typhoid!"

Lord Sheldon's eyes were on her face and there was an expression in them which, had she not been looking away from him, she would have recognised.

But the carriage was approaching Flagstaff House

and ahead of them were sentries outside the gates.

"I want you to go to bed as soon as you get back," Lord Sheldon said. "You have been through a very frightening and tiring experience. I will talk to your Uncle. Go straight upstairs and go to sleep, Azalea. Everything will be all right tomorrow."

She did not answer, but he knew she was afraid.

Some instinctive mechanism within him told him that her secret was connected with her father.

In all his adventurous and, at times, desperately dangerous career Lord Sheldon had always trusted his instinct and it had never failed him.

Whenever it had seemed that everything had gone wrong, that the problem was insoluble or a position untenable, he had always been able to draw upon an inner strength and a power on which he relied to give him the assistance he needed.

He was sure now that he could solve Azalea's secret and assuage her fears.

He was certain, as he had never been certain of anything in the whole of his life before, that she would become his wife because they were meant for each other.

The carriage drew up at Flagstaff House and as the footman stepped down to open the door Lord Sheldon said again:

"Do exactly what I tell you, Azalea. Go straight upstairs to your room."

She looked up at him, her eyes very dark and frightened.

"I love . . . you!" she whispered, then turned away and stepped out of the carriage.

Chapter Seven

As Azalea crossed the Hall and ran up the broad staircase she knew that the servants looked at her in surprise and that one of the Aides-de-Camp coming out of a Sitting-Room had also caught sight of her.

She was well aware that to them she must look extraordinary in her Chinese costume.

She could only hope that Lord Sheldon would find some plausible excuse which would not infuriate her Uncle even more than the knowledge that she had been on a Chinese junk.

When she reached her bed-room she locked the door behind her, feeling somehow it would protect her against the storm which she knew would be brewing downstairs.

Now the consequences of her actions began to come home with a vengeance!

There were the explanations she must contrive to make, and she began to tremble at the thought of what both her Uncle and Aunt would say when they learnt that she had made friends with Mr. and Mrs. Chang and had actually accompanied them out to sea.

But more insistent in her mind than the thought of her Uncle and Aunt's anger at her being friendly with the Chinese was the problem of Lord Sheldon.

It seemed impossible, now that she was alone, for her to realise that he had actually asked her to marry him.

Deep in her heart she supposed she had always

prayed—but blindly and without hope—that he might care for her because she loved him so desperately.

But she had been quite certain that he would never stoop to marrying someone as unimportant as herself, who was overshadowed with the secret that grew into horrifying proportions whenever she thought of it.

How could any man in his position want a wife who lived under a dark cloud and could not even tell him the reason for it?

But he really had asked her to marry him, and she felt herself quiver at the wonder of it even while she knew it was hopeless.

But he had said he was never defeated and always got his own way!

Azalea walked across the room to stand at the window looking out over the trees to where in the distance there was the blue of the sea against the dark green of Kowloon.

Beyond again were the mountain-peaks of China illuminated with the brilliant red and gold of the setting sun, and seeming in their glory a fitting place to be the abode of Gods and Goddesses.

It was so beautiful, so lovely!

Quite suddenly it gave Azalea a new courage and a bravery she had not possessed before.

Why, she asked herself, should she be denied everything in her life that was beautiful? Why should she deliberately submit herself to her Uncle's ruling and accept his decree that she must not marry?

She knew that both her father and her mother had wanted her happiness above all else.

She knew too that her mother would never have allowed herself to be humiliated and trodden underfoot by the General.

She could hear her mother in the past laughing at the pomposity and the pretensions of Senior Officials and their wives who imagined themselves to be too grand to condescend to the wives of junior Officers or even to the Officers themselves.

She would amuse Azalea and her father when she mimicked the manner in which they spoke; the way in which the women would sweep into a room as if they were Queens or Empresses rather than merely the wife of a General or of the Governor of a Province, whose importance only lasted the five years he was in office.

"They are a lot of sacred cows!" Azalea once heard her mother say, "and because we are bemused by the importance they assume for themselves, we are too frightened to remember that when they return home to England they will retire into obscurity, and no-one will listen to their long, rambling tales of India!"

"You are right, my darling!" Azalea's father had said, "but if you express such revolutionary statements too loudly, I shall be cashiered for impudence!"

"Then we will retire to the Himalayas!" Azalea's mother had said with a little laugh, "where we will sit and talk with the wise sadhus, the Yogis, and the fakirs, and we will learn about the really important things of life."

"The really important thing as far as I am concerned," Azalea's father replied, "is that I love you! Whatever people do outside this house, we are complete in ourselves and they cannot hurt us."

But that had not been true!

Because of Colonel Stewart's brutality, her father had been forced to take his own life, and before that her mother had died of cholera because she had tried to help one of their servants who was ill and had picked up the deadly infection in the Bazaar.

"Mama would have stood up to Uncle Frederick," Azalea told herself now.

And she knew that she must not let the wonder and the beauty of her love for Lord Sheldon slip away from her by behaving like a coward.

She turned from the window, and because he had told her to do so she undressed and got into bed.

Only as she sank back against the pillows did she realise that in actual fact she was very exhausted.

The fear she had experienced when the junk was attacked, the terror of being carried aboard the pirate-ship, and the anticipation of what awaited her and Kai Yin if they were sold had left her drained emotionally.

And yet, as if it were a star shining over her head, she could recall so vividly Lord Sheldon's words when he had said:

"How soon will you marry me, my precious?"

Even to think about it made a little quiver of delight run through Azalea, and she shut her eyes to imagine that he was holding her in his arms and his lips were seeking hers.

"I love him! I love him!" she whispered.

And knew that the love she had for him was something so deep and so fundamental that she did in fact belong to him completely and absolutely.

"If I never saw him again," she told herself, "no other man could ever mean anything in my life."

She had known that her mother with her strange Russian mysticism had loved her father in the same way.

It was a love that could happen once in a lifetime and for only one man.

'I am the same,' Azalea thought. 'I shall love him until I die and there can never be anyone else.'

She was almost asleep when she heard a knock on her door.

For a moment she thought she must have dreamt it, then as she listened it came again.

"Who is it?" she asked, remembering that she had locked herself in.

"I wish to speak with you, Azalea."

There was no mistaking the harshness of her Uncle's tone. Azalea sat up wide awake and conscious that her heart was beating violently and feeling a sudden dryness in her mouth.

"I . . . I am . . . in bed . . . Uncle Frederick," she said after a moment.

"Open the door!"

It was a command, and drawing in her breath Azalea rose slowly from the bed. Picking up a thin cotton wrapper which lay over a chair, she put it on and tied the sash round her slim waist.

Slowly, as if she had to force her feet to obey her,

she walked towards the door, turned the key, and opened it.

The General was standing outside.

He seemed big and overpowering in his uniform with his medals on his breast, his gold insignia glittering in the last faint rays of the setting sun coming through the window.

He walked into the room and closed the door behind him.

Azalea backed a little way away from him to wait apprehensively. Then he said:

"I presume it is no use asking you for an explanation of your disgraceful behaviour?"

"I am . . . sorry . . . Uncle Frederick," Azalea said.

Her voice seemed very quiet and low in contrast to his hectoring tones.

"Sorry? Is that all you have to say?" her Uncle asked. "How dare you, as a guest in my house, consort with Chinese! Where did you meet these people?"

"On . . . board . . . the *Orissa.*"

"And you visited them knowing I would disapprove?"

"They were . . . friends of mine."

"Friends!" the General snorted. "How can you be friends with Chinese, especially knowing my position here in Hong Kong and what I feel about the Governor entertaining them?"

"I feel the . . . same as he . . . does," Azalea said.

Her face was very pale, but her eyes, which she kept on her Uncle's face, were brave and her expression showed none of the nervous tumult within her.

"How dare you speak to me in such a way!" the General shouted.

Reaching out his right hand, he slapped Azalea hard across the cheek.

She staggered, gave an involuntary little cry, and put one hand up to her face.

"After all I have done for you," the General stormed, "taking you into my house, acknowledging you as my niece, even though I was ashamed and humiliated by your father's murderous action and your mother's Russian blood."

He paused and then he added:

"I might have expected from the child of such a marriage that you should associate with Orientals, that you should degrade yourself by wearing their costume and involve me in a scandal that will reverberate from Hong Kong to London!"

Again the General paused as if to catch his breath.

"Can you imagine what will be said when it is learnt that my niece, living in my house sneaked away on a Chinese junk to get herself captured by pirates and rescued unfortunately by the British Navy?"

He emphasised the word "unfortunately." Then, as if Azalea had questioned him, he went on:

"Yes, I mean unfortunately! It would have been better, far better, if the pirates had either drowned you because you were British or sold you into slavery. It is what you deserve!"

The General spoke so violently, almost spitting the words at her, that instinctively Azalea took a step backwards.

Then he said:

"Not content with making a fool of me, you have dared to disobey the restrictions I laid upon you when you first came back from India. Do you remember what I said?"

Azalea tried to answer but no words would come to her lips.

Her cheek was burning from the violence of her Uncle's blow. She was trembling but she hoped he was not aware of it.

"I told you," the General continued, "that you would never be allowed to marry; that I would never give my permission for any man to make you his wife! Yet you have dared—dared in your perfidy—to encourage Lord Sheldon!"

For the first time since he had entered the room Azalea dropped her eyes.

She could not bear to look at her Uncle's red face,

contorted with anger, and listen to what she knew he was going to say.

"Did you really think," he asked, "that I would alter my determination to ensure that the secret of your father's crime goes with you to the grave?"

He raised his voice as he stormed:

"Never!—and I mean never, Azalea—will I permit any man to know of this blot on the family honour. I believed, foolishly, I now admit, that you understood why you must obey me."

Azalea found her voice.

"B-but I . . . want to marry Lord Sheldon. I love him and he . . . loves me."

The General gave a short laugh and it was an ugly sound.

"Love? What do you know of love?" he asked. "As for Sheldon, he must be raving mad to want you as his wife! The only asset you have is that you are my niece, and as your Uncle and your Guardian I have refused your importunate lover."

"No! No!" Azalea cried. "I cannot permit you to do this to me. I wish to marry him."

"Apparently, God help him, he wishes to marry you!" the General sneered. "But let me tell you, Azalea, it is something that will never happen!"

"Why not? Why should you prevent it?" Azalea asked with a sudden burst of courage. "It is unjust! Papa paid the penalty for what was an unfortunate accident. Why should I be punished for something that had nothing to do with me? I have a right to be married . . . like any other woman . . . to the man I . . . love!"

As Azalea spoke, the words came from her lips positively and with a determination she had never shown before. She knew that she was fighting not only for her own happiness but also for Lord Sheldon's.

"So you are determined to defy me?" her Uncle asked.

Now his voice was lower, but it seemed to be more menacing.

"I wish to marry . . . Lord Sheldon!"

He looked at her speculatively and his lips tightened.

"I have told Sheldon I will not permit it," the General said, "but he will not take no for an answer. You will therefore, Azalea, sit down at that table and write to him saying that you refuse to marry him and have no wish to see him again."

"You want me to ... write ... that?" Azalea asked incredulously.

"I order you to do so!"

"I refuse. I will not write lies, not even to please you! I want to marry him ... I want to see him again ... I love him!"

"And I intend that you shall obey me," the General said firmly. "Will you write that letter, Azalea, or must I force you to do so?"

Azalea threw up her head.

"You will never make me write it," she answered defiantly.

"Very well," the General replied, "if you will not acquiesce willingly in what I ask of you, then I will exact your obedience by other methods!"

He moved as he spoke and for the first time Azalea saw that he carried in his left hand a long, thin riding-whip.

It was one that he always used on his horses.

She looked at it and her expression was incredulous! Yet her eyes asked the question that she could not put into words.

"I have never beaten my daughters," the General said, "because there has been no necessity for me to do so. But had there been, I should have had no compunction about flogging them, as I was flogged as a boy, and as I would flog my son, if I had one."

He transferred the whip into his right hand. Then he said sternly:

"I give you one more chance. Will you write that letter, or shall I force you to do so?"

"I will never ... write it, whatever you ... do to me!" Azalea replied.

But she gave a little scream as unexpectedly the

General took hold of the back of her neck and threw her face-downwards onto the bed.

For a moment she thought: 'This cannot be happening!' Then the whip seared its way like a sharp knife across her back and again she opened her mouth to scream.

But with a superhuman effort at self-control she pressed her lips together.

She would not acknowledge the pain of it! She would not give in, whatever he did to her!

The whip fell again and again, biting through the thin cotton of her wrapper and the muslin of her night-gown.

They gave her no protection, and as the General brought the wiry, flexible instrument of torture down upon her the pain grew more and more unbearable.

Azalea began to feel as if her will, and even her identity, was being thrashed away from her.

She was no longer herself. She could no longer think. She could only wince with the agony of one blow and wait apprehensively for the next.

She felt as if her whole body were dissolving into a pain that spread from her neck to her knees; a pain that grew and grew until at last she heard someone screaming and wondered who it could be.

Then mercifully the pain ceased and as if his voice came from a long distance away she heard her Uncle ask:

"Now will you do what I tell you?"

It was impossible for her to reply and after a moment he said, his voice hard and harsh:

"You will write that letter, or I shall continue to beat you. It is your choice, Azalea."

She wanted to tell him that she would never write it; but for the moment it was impossible to speak, difficult to remember what the letter was about or even to whom she had to write it.

The whip fell again and now it jerked a piercing scream from her lips.

"Will you write the letter?"

Azalea felt the whip would cut her in pieces, that she would sink through the bed and onto the floor.

"I . . . I . . . will . . . write . . . it."

The words came gasping from between her lips because she knew she could bear no more.

Her whole body felt as if it were an open sore and the pain, as she tried to raise herself, was agonising.

Her Uncle took her roughly by the arm and pulled her to her feet.

"Go to the writing-table."

Stumbling, holding on to the furniture for support, Azalea reached the writing-table which was in the window.

Somehow she managed to sit down on the chair and stare stupidly at the blotter, her hands shaking, her face wet with tears, although she was not aware that she was crying.

Impatiently her Uncle opened the blotter and set a piece of writing-paper in front of her. He dipped the nib of the pen into the ink and placed it between her fingers.

"Write what I tell you."

Azalea's fingers were trembling so that it was difficult to grip the pen.

"Dear Lord Sheldon," her Uncle dictated.

Because her brain felt numb, because she felt as if life had almost left her body, Azalea did as she was told.

Painstakingly she wrote the three words.

"I have no wish to accept your offer of marriage . . ." Sir Frederick dictated, and waited while Azalea inscribed the words, "and I never want to see you again."

Azalea put down the pen.

"No!" she said in a voice that trembled. "I cannot . . . write that! It is . . . not true. I . . . I wish to . . . marry him. I . . . do . . . want to see . . . him."

In answer the General brought the whip he still held in his hand down violently upon the writing-table.

The ink-pot rattled and so did the tray containing the pens.

"You wish to be beaten until you do agree?" he answered. "Make no mistake about this, Azalea, I shall not have the slightest compunction about beating you not once, but two or three times a day, until this letter is written, and until then you will have nothing to eat or drink."

He looked down at her tear-stained face and trembling hands.

"How long do you imagine you can defy me?" he asked contemptuously.

Azalea knew there was nothing she could do.

Her whole being shrank in terror from being forced to bear further pain.

The weals on her back were throbbing intolerably and even to move her hand was agony. She was defeated and she knew it.

She picked up the pen, and although her writing looked as if a spider had crawled across the page, she wrote the words that her Uncle required.

"Sign your name!" the General commanded.

She signed and he lifted the paper from the blotter.

Without speaking he picked up his whip and walked across the room to the door. Taking the key from the lock, he went from the room.

Azalea heard herself being locked in. Then like a hunted animal she crept back into bed and hid her face in the pillow.

The pain of her body prevented Azalea from sleeping until after the dawn had crept up the sky, lighting the darkness of her room.

Then she must have dozed a short while because she awoke with a start to hear the door open.

She looked with terror to see who was approaching the bed, afraid that it might be her Uncle.

But it was a Chinese maid who stood there, an elderly woman who had been on the staff of Flagstaff House for many years and had served under many successive Generals.

"Me Lady say Missy get up at once," she said in her lilting voice.

"Get up?" Azalea asked in surprise. "What time is it?"

"Five o'clock, Missy."

"Why am I to get up?" Azalea enquired.

"Missy go 'way," the Chinese woman replied. "I pack few things for Missy in bag."

Azalea tried to sit up in bed and gave a groan of anguish from the pain it caused her back, which had now stiffened.

"I do not . . . understand," she said after a moment.

"Missy best get up," the Chinese maid advised, "or Me-Lady be angry."

Azalea was certain that the maid could give her no more information that she had received.

At the same time, it was puzzling that her Aunt should wish her to rise so early, and Azalea wondered where she could be sending her.

Perhaps she was to go back to England, in which case, she thought, she would be able to find Lord Sheldon again when he returned home.

She was quite certain he would not be satisfied with the note she had written him or believe that she had written it of her own free will.

But she could not help wondering what her Uncle had said to him and whether he had painted so black a picture of her that Lord Sheldon might be influenced by it.

Then she told herself that he loved her even as she loved him and would not believe anything which was said about her.

She was sure of his love.

With difficulty, because every movement was an agony in itself. Azalea got dressed, finding that her whale-bone corsets were like instruments of inquisition. But she dared not risk her Aunt's rage should she omit them.

The weals on her waist from her Uncle's whip made the tight band of her petticoat seem intolerable and it hurt even to put her arms into her gown and wait while the maid buttoned it.

She arranged her hair in a tight chignon and, because she felt her Aunt would expect it, she put on a small plain hat which tied with ribbons under her chin.

While she was dressing the Chinese maid put some of her underclothes in a small valise and added her brushes and combs, her washing materials, her wrapper, and bed-room slippers.

"What about gowns?" Azalea asked.

The Chinese maid shook her head.

"Me-Lady say these only things I to pack in bag. Nothing else."

Azalea was puzzled.

Surely her Aunt would not expect her to return home on a ship with only one gown to wear for the whole of the voyage?

And if she was not going back to England, then where could she be going?

As Azalea picked up her gloves and her handbag the maid went from the room to return almost immediately.

"Come! Me-Lady waits!"

Wondering what could be happening, Azalea went down the passage to find her Aunt waiting for her outside her bed-room.

One look at her face was enough to tell Azalea how angry she was.

"Where are we going, Aunt Emily?"

"You will learn that when we get there," her Aunt replied. "I do not wish to speak to you, Azalea. I am disgusted by your behaviour and since we must travel together it will be in silence."

"Very well, Aunt Emily," Azalea said. "But . . ."

Before she could say any more Lady Osmund had walked ahead and was preceding her down the stairs.

As she followed Azalea could see that outside the front door there was a closed carriage.

Quite suddenly she was frightened. Something was happening she did not understand. Where were they taking her? How would Lord Sheldon find her?

She had a wild impulse to run away; to refuse to get into the carriage; to run away down the drive; perhaps to go to the Changs' house and ask them to protect her.

But she knew that her Uncle would have every right to fetch her back and that he would in fact not hesitate to do so.

She could not involve the Changs in this unpleasantness, and besides she had a feeling that long before she could reach them the servants would be ordered to overtake her and drag her back, forcibly if necessary, to Flagstaff House.

It was impossible to contemplate such humiliation and, apart from anything else, owing to the pain of her back Azalea was almost certain she would not be able to run very far.

Her Aunt had reached the Hall.

There were several Chinese servants in attendance. Suddenly Azalea saw that Ah Yok was holding open the carriage door.

She realised at once that here was her only chance to communicate with Lord Sheldon.

What could she say? What could she tell him?

Then as Azalea reached the front door she saw on the lowest step a spot of blue.

Because it was so early the steps had not yet been scrubbed as they were every morning, and the Blue Magpie's feather must have fallen from its wings as a bird flew over the house.

Azalea bent down and picked it up.

Her Aunt was already stepping into the carriage and Azalea, putting the feather into Ah Yok's hand, tried wildly to remember the Cantonese word for "Nobleman."

She could not remember it, so instead she whispered

"Give to English Mandarin."

Ah Yok's hand closed over the feather and he nodded without speaking.

Azalea's voice had been very low but as she seated herself in the carriage beside her Aunt, Lady Osmund said:

"What did you say to that servant?"

The carriage door was shut and they were proceeding down the drive.

"I . . . I said . . . good-bye," Azalea answered hesitatingly.

"In Chinese?" her Aunt asked.

She was carrying a fan in her hand and she slapped Azalea with it on the side of her face.

"You have no right to speak to the servants in any language but English!" she said. "Has your Uncle not punished you enough for running after the Chinese, for wishing to associate with them?"

Azalea did not answer. Her Aunt had struck her in the same place that her Uncle had slapped her the night before and it hurt intolerably.

Lady Osmund did not speak again.

As the horses trotted down the hill, Azalea realised they were nearing the sea, but proceeding in a direction away from Old Praya.

Ahead she saw what she knew was a jetty used by the Military launches, and that one was waiting for them, the sailors in their white uniforms standing by the gang-plank.

Lady Osmund descended from the carriage and Azalea followed her down the jetty.

They stepped aboard the Military launch and she noticed, and was quite certain it was intentional, that there was no British Officer in charge, only a Chinese.

'Where are they taking me? Where can we be going?' she wondered frantically.

The gang-plank was taken aboard and the engines began to turn as the launch set out into the blue waters of the harbour.

Azalea realised they were heading West and as they passed several islands she longed to ask where they were going, but did not dare interrupt her Aunt's stony silence.

Lady Osmund sat upright in the launch, taking apparently no interest in the view or the islands as they steamed past them. One hand was gripped tightly round the ivory handle of her sunshade.

She fanned herself occasionally but otherwise made

no movement, and because she was certain she would get no answer to any question she might ask, Azalea also was silent.

She could, however, hear the sailors chattering outside and understood some of the words they spoke.

She listened attentively and thought that one of them said something that sounded like "four hours."

If they were to travel for four hours, where could they be going?

They had left Flagstaff House soon after five-thirty, which meant, Azalea reckoned, that in four hours it would still be only nine-thirty.

Then she heard one of the sailors say a word she recognised and knew the answer!

Macao!

She had read about the Portuguese Colony of Macao which lay on the Western side of the mouth of the Pearl River estuary.

She was almost certain it was about forty miles from Hong Kong, and she remembered reading that it was the oldest European outpost on the China coast, a Portuguese settlement and Roman Catholic Bishopric.

It was one of the places Azalea had hoped to visit while she was in Hong Kong because there had been a great deal about it in the history-book that she had read, which had described many of the beautiful buildings.

But she had thought it unlikely that she would ever have the chance since her Uncle would have no official duties there, and her Aunt would certainly not wish to go sight-seeing.

But if that was their destination now, why should she be taken to Macao?

She tried desperately to remember more of what she had read and was almost certain that Macao was connected with gambling, which could not have anything to do with her.

'What else is there?' she questioned, and could find no answer.

The sun was rising and it was growing much hotter.

Her Aunt fanned herself vigorously and Azalea

wished that she too had thought to bring a fan with her.

Nevertheless, she liked the heat; it was the burning mark on her cheek which was causing her pain and the intolerable throbbing of her back which seemed to get worse as the hours passed by.

Then suddenly there was the yellowish water of the Pearl River, full of sediment and very different from the clear, deep ocean water which bathed Hong Kong.

There was a slight swell which would not have been enough to disturb most people, but Lady Osmund brought out a bottle of smelling-salts from her bag and Azalea wondered whether she would be sick.

Then ahead a narrow harbour came into sight, and above it the towers of Churches. There were many trees in full blossom in front of the beautiful baroque Eighteenth-Century Portuguese houses.

The launch reached the jetty and Lady Osmund stepped ashore without even glancing at Azalea.

She followed, almost like a dog, she thought to herself.

There was a closed carriage waiting for them and when they were seated the horses started off, and Azalea said with a desperate note in her voice:

"You must tell me, Aunt Emily, why we have come here! I have to know!"

Lady Osmund did not answer but because she was suddenly very afraid, Azalea insisted:

"If you do not answer me I shall jump out of the carriage here and now and run away."

"You will do nothing of the sort," Lady Osmund said, breaking her silence of over four hours.

"Then where are we going?" Azalea asked.

"I am taking you to a place where you will be taught to behave as I apparently have been unable to teach you," Lady Osmund said with a note of spite in her voice.

"But what is it?" Azalea asked. "What sort of place?"

"Your Uncle and I have considered what is best for you and for us," Lady Osmund answered. "We have tried to do our duty, Azalea, but you have repaid us with gross ingratitude. Now we have to take firmer steps to see that what occurred yesterday will not occur again."

"But you still have not answered my question," Azalea said. "Where am I to live—and why Macao?"

As she spoke the carriage, which had been climbing the hill, came to a standstill.

Azalea, who had been looking at her Aunt, turned her head and looked out the window.

She saw a high wall, a huge doorway with an iron-studded door, and in the centre of it a grill.

She thought for a moment that it was a Church, then as she stared, trying to understand, Lady Osmund said:

"This, Azalea, is the Convent of the Penitent Sisters of Mary."

"A Convent?" Azalea exclaimed.

She was so astonished that she was unable to say any more as her Aunt descended from the carriage.

They were obviously expected; for before the bell could be rung the door was opened by a Nun.

"I wish to see the Mother Superior," Lady Osmund said.

"She is expecting you," the Nun answered in broken English.

Azalea wondered for one moment if she should run away now, but before she could make up her mind the heavy door had closed behind them and they were proceeding down a long, flagged passage with the Nun leading the way.

She was a very old woman, and judging by her appearance and the sound of her voice Azalea guessed she must be Portuguese.

They walked a long way, their feet seeming to echo in the cool quietness of the passage.

They passed a court-yard that was full of green plants, then on again along passages white-washed and empty of all furniture.

At last the Nun stopped before a high door and knocked.

A voice bade her in Portuguese to enter and the door was opened.

In a square room furnished only with several high-backed chairs, a plain oak table, and a huge crucifix on the wall was an elderly Nun dressed all in white, with a rosary hanging from her waist.

"You are the Mother Superior?" Lady Osmund asked in English.

"I am, Lady Osmund," the Nun answered in the same language. "Will Your Ladyship sit down?"

Lady Osmund sat down in front of the table.

The Nun made a little gesture with her hand towards Azalea, who sat on another chair.

"You received General Sir Frederick Osmund's letter?" Lady Osmund asked.

"The message arrived after midnight," the Mother Superior replied, "and as the Sister on duty gathered it was urgent, she brought it straight to me."

"It was in fact very urgent," Lady Osmund said. "I think Sir Frederick made it very clear what we require."

"I understood from his letter," the Mother Superior said, "that you wish your niece, after instruction, to take the final vows."

"That is our wish," Lady Osmund said firmly.

"No!" Azalea cried. "If that is what you have planned for me, Aunt Emily, I will not agree! I will not become a Nun!"

It was frightening that neither the Mother Superior nor Lady Osmund even looked at her; they just ignored her outburst.

"As Sir Frederick will have explained," Lady Osmund said, "there is no other course where this girl is concerned. He has, I am sure, spoken of her misdemeanours and the fact that she is beyond our control?"

"Sir Frederick wrote very fully," the Mother Superior answered.

"Then I feel I can leave her in your hands," Lady Osmund said. "You have a reputation, I believe, for dealing with young women who are in need of correction?"

"We have been successful in many instances," the Mother Superior agreed.

"Then may I say that my husband and I are deeply grateful to you for taking this girl in your charge. We feel sure she will be brought to a better state of mind than we have been successful in creating."

"And we are grateful," the Mother Superior said, "for the dowry which Sir Frederick enclosed, and which will be used for the good of our Order."

"You understand," Lady Osmund said, "that we have no wish ever to hear of this girl again. It is, I believe, unnecessary for her to keep her own name, nor will it be recorded in your Register."

"That is correct," the Mother Superior answered. "We are an enclosed Order. Your niece will be baptised into the Catholic faith with a name we will choose for her. Her surname will cease to exist from that moment. She will thereafter be addressed only as she has been newly christened."

Azalea looked from one to the other.

She could not believe that what she was hearing was true. It was impossible that they should be planning her whole life, her whole future, in these few sentences!

She rose to her feet, and as she would have run towards the door the Mother Superior said in a tone of authority:

"If you try to run away you will be forcibly restrained."

Azalea paused and turned back, her face very pale, her eyes enormous.

"I cannot stay here," she said. "I do not wish to become a Nun, and I will not be a Catholic!"

"God and your Guardians know what is best for you."

"But it is not best," Azalea said. "I have no desire to be confined here."

Lady Osmund rose to her feet.

"This is very distressing and unnecessary," she said. "My husband and I have done our duty. We can do no more. I leave this girl and her wickedness entirely in your hands."

"I understand," the Mother Superior said, "and I promise you that we shall pray for her and for you also, My Lady."

"Thank you," Lady Osmund replied with dignity.

She walked towards the door, passing Azalea as she did so, but she did not even look at her.

The door was opened before she could touch it and Azalea knew that the Nun outside had been waiting for her to leave.

She turned towards the Mother Superior.

"Please listen to me," she pleaded, "please let me ... explain what has happened and why I have been ... brought here."

"There will be plenty of time later for me to hear all you have to say," the Mother Superior answered. "Now I want you to come with me."

She walked from the room and because there was nothing else she could do Azalea followed her.

There were several Nuns waiting outside in the passage and she had the feeling that they were there to prevent her from running away and force her, if necessary, to behave as they wished.

Again there was a long walk down vast, empty corridors until they came to a row of doors, each with a grid in its centre. Azalea was sure they were the Nuns' cells.

A Sister carrying a key hurried forward to open one of the doors.

It was the tinest room Azalea had ever seen!

There was one window very high up which had a view only of the sky. There was a wooden bed and a ewer and basin on a deal-table. There was one hard chair and on the wall a crucifix.

"This is your cell," the Mother Superior said.

"But I want to say . . ." Azalea began.

"I have heard of your behaviour," the Mother Superior interrupted, "and I know how deeply you have distressed those who have tried to be kind to you. Because of what I have learnt, I want to give you time to think about your sins and to repent of them. You will see no-one for six days."

Her expression was severe as she went on:

"Your food will be brought to you, but you will have no communication with anyone outside this cell. Once a day you will be taken to a court-yard for exercise. After that you will continue to meditate on your sins and your immortal soul. Then I will see you again."

As she finished speaking the Mother Superior went from the cell and the door closed behind her.

There was the click of the key turning in the lock, then the sound of the Nuns' footsteps as they walked away down the corridor.

Azalea listened until they faded into the distance.

Then there was only silence—a silence in which she could hear her heart breaking.

Chapter Eight

"I have been here for five days," Azalea said to herself as the sun rose to illuminate her bare cell with a glimmer of gold.

It might have been five months, five years, or even five centuries.

She felt as if she had ceased to exist, as if she were living in a void where there was no time and no future.

The first night, when she had been left alone in the cell, she had cried desperately, conscious that she was not only frightened but also losing hope.

How could she ever be saved, ever be rescued from this prison that was more inviolable than any gaol could be?

She knew that the Nuns who entered enclosed Orders were forgotten by the world, and once they passed through the door of the Convent they had no further contact with their relations or their friends.

Her Uncle and Aunt had been very clever, Azalea thought, in removing her so quickly from Hong Kong and incarcerating her here.

It would, she was certain, be quite impossible for Lord Sheldon to find her.

Even if he disbelieved the letter she had been forced to write to him, even if he received the feather of the Blue Magpie she had handed to Ah Yok, he would still be up against an impenetrable wall of secrecy.

Azalea was quite certain that where the Nuns were concerned there would be no gossip.

The Mother Superior would make sure that she became anonymous, as her Uncle and Aunt wished, and Azalea feared despairingly that sooner or later they would wear down her resistance: she would become a Catholic, and take her final vows simply because there was no alternative.

Her day began at five o'clock when a bell clanged in the Convent, echoing down the empty passages.

She would hear the Nuns hurrying along to what she knew was a call for the first Service of the day.

Far away in the distance she would hear them chanting and their voices intoning the prayers.

At six o'clock her cell door was opened and an elderly Nun brought her a broom and a bucket with which she cleaned her cell.

The Nun did not speak. She only made it obvious what she expected and Azalea found that every other day she had to go down on her knees and scrub the bare boards.

The first morning after she had been awakened the same Nun had taken away her clothes and left in their stead a black cotton habit, so shapeless and ugly that Azalea had looked at it in horror.

There were coarse calico underclothes to wear beneath, rough and unbleached so that with every movement they hurt the soreness of her bruised and swollen back.

The night-gown they had given her had been of the same material, and after spending an intolerable hour in it Azalea had taken it off and crept back into bed naked.

Thick cotton stockings and serviceable leather shoes completed the outfit, and a postulant's veil of thin black material covered her hair and fastened at the nape of her neck.

Since there was no mirror in the cell, Azalea could not see herself; but she was well aware of what she must look like and she thought with a little sob that, dressed as she was now, no-one would call her "Fragrant Flower."

The elderly Nun intimated that she must draw back her hair in a tight bun at the back of her head, and as she obeyed the unspoken order, Azalea remembered that when she took her vows her hair would be cut off and her head shaved!

Every feminine instinct in her body revolted at the thought!

When the cell was cleaned to the satisfaction of the Nun watching her, food was put inside the door and Azalea was left alone.

At first she decided that she would not eat, then sheer hunger forced her to accept what was brought with monotonous regularity.

For breakfast there was the coarse dark bread that peasants commonly ate in Europe and which Azalea knew was nourishing. With it came a small slice of goat's cheese, and one day a few black olives.

At ten o'clock the Nuns attended Chapel again and Azalea could hear them chanting for what seemed to her a long time.

At eleven o'clock it was time for exercise and Azalea was taken from her cell into a small court-yard.

The walls rose high on two sides of it and on the top of them Azalea could see there were spikes of jagged glass which glittered in the sunshine like jewels, but which would be exceedingly dangerous to anyone who attempted to scale them.

The walls were very high and menacing and there were no trees near them.

Azalea, looking at them speculatively, knew that it would be impossible for anyone to climb them, however agile he might be.

The court-yard contained no flowers, but there were some shrubs which grew wild and luxuriant, similar to those she had seen in Hong Kong, and these were in bloom.

They had small white blossoms not unlike a lilac, and there was a faint scent about them. Otherwise the court-yard was severe and ugly, and the grass, although it was early in the season, was already browning in the heat of the sun.

Azalea wondered if perhaps it was part of her punishment that there was to be only austerity and ugliness about her and that beauty was another worldly pleasure which was forbidden.

At exactly half-past eleven o'clock she was taken back to her cell and locked in. There was then nothing to do but wait until the second meal of the day was brought to her at noon.

This consisted of a soup, sometimes containing fish, but mostly of vegetables that Azalea did not recognise, and with it a small bowl of rice.

The same ingredients appeared for supper at six o'clock, and the hours in between seemed interminable.

If only they would allow her books, Azalea thought, she would have been able to read and think of something else besides her own misery.

But she knew it was part of the plan that she should, as the Mother Superior had said, meditate upon her "sins and repent of them."

She decided with the last flickering embers of her defiance she would never repent of having loved Lord Sheldon.

She would sit thinking of him, sending her thoughts winging towards him.

She imagined them being carried over the sea between Macao and Hong Kong, so that perhaps he would think of her and wonder where she could be and how he could see her again.

At night Azalea would imagine that his arms were around her and his lips were on hers.

Sometimes she would feel a little flicker of the [ ] he had awoken in her re-echoing in her breast. T[ ] she would remember miserably that this was all [ ] would have to sustain her through the long : ahead, and she wanted only to die.

Kai Yin Chang had been ready to kill herself rather than be defamed, but Azalea thought helplessly that there was no way that she could do the same.

Besides she could not help remembering how she had told Kai Yin that it was wrong and wicked to take one's own life, and that the British always believed that 'where there was life there was hope!'

Sometimes when the night seemed very long and

dark she would tell herself a story in which Lord
Sheldon climbed over the wall when she was walking in
the court-yard and carried her away to safety.

But her practical mind told her that this was impossible.

Besides, she was certain that even if she could haul
herself up on a rope and avoid the sharp points of
glass on the top of the wall, someone looking through
the windows of the Convent was bound to notice her.

"Oh, God, save me!" Azalea prayed night after
night and day after day. "You saved me once when it
seemed impossible by bringing Lord Sheldon to my
rescue. Save me now from a life that would be . . .
worse than . . . death!"

Sometimes she wanted to scream, to beat her hands
against the door of her cell, as she felt the walls were
closing in on her and she was being suffocated by
them.

She told herself it was her Russian blood that was
making her feel so wild and unrestrained.

Her father had always been self-controlled and, except when he had been forced to take action against
the brutality of Colonel Stewart to save a young girl,
he had a reserve and a pride that would never have allowed him to give way to emotionalism.

"You were brave, Papa!" Azalea found herself saying to him in the darkness, "brave enough to stop a
man who was behaving in a bestial fashion."

She gave a little sob as she continued in a whisper:

"You were also brave enough to shoot yourself because it was the right and honourable thing to do."

Then desperately, in a voice that pierced the
darkness, Azalea cried:

"Help me, Papa! Help me now, for I cannot endure
this . . . I cannot!"

After three or four days the scars on her back, although tender, ceased to be so painful and she could
even lie comfortably in bed.

She knew that her Uncle had inflicted on her not
only what he thought of as just punishment for her be-

haviour but also his resentment against her father and the scandal he feared.

Azalea wondered whether, if she had gone on fighting him as she had wanted to do, in fact he would have beaten her insensible because he was so determined to get his own way.

Although she might despise herself for having given in so easily, she knew that the end was inevitable, for she could not have resisted indefinitely.

After several more beatings she would have capitulated ignominiously because both physically and mentally she would have been unable to stand any more.

Sometimes she would walk up and down her cell because she felt so restless she could neither sit nor lie.

"I am like a caged animal!" she told herself.

Then she remembered that sooner or later in captivity even the fiercest animal became cowed, intimidated, and finally apathetic.

"How long will it be before I no longer care?" she asked.

But she was sure that the thought of Lord Sheldon would always bring that dagger-like pain to her heart and an agonising torture to her mind.

"I love him! I love him!" she whispered.

Yet she wondered if the day would come when the words would have no meaning; when even the ecstasy of remembering him would fade and be forgotten.

Although the silence and the fact that she was always alone was frightening and at times intolerable, Azalea could not help feeling that when the week was over it might be even worse.

Then she was quite certain her religious instruction would begin. Gradually they would wear away her will and her critical faculties so that she would accept what she was told and become the automaton they desired.

When as usual the Nun arrived at ten o'clock with a brush and pail for Azalea to clean her cell, she did what was expected of her automatically, and when the Nun left she waited listlessly for another half hour before it was time for her exercise.

She looked forward to being outside just because the

air was fresher than it was in her cell and at least she could feel the warmth of the sun on her head.

She knew that beyond the walls there was the sea, blue against the green of the mountains, but she also knew despairingly that she would never see it again.

Her only glimpse of the world she had found so beautiful would be the sky, sometimes blue, sometimes grey and overcast, and at others, as it was this morning, translucent in the golden sun and shimmering with the promise of heat later in the day.

She looked up hoping to see a bird, but the sky was empty and she wondered if perhaps even they too would be forbidden to her.

She remembered the yellow-green South China White-Eye which the shop-keepers kept in cages to make their customers feel happy, and she recalled the flight of Blue Magpies which had risen in Mr. Chang's garden when she and Lord Sheldon had stepped out onto the verandah.

"I thought they would bring me luck!" Azalea told herself miserably.

As she thought of the Magpies she saw at the end of the court-yard a patch of vivid blue on the rough green grass.

Wonderingly she walked towards it and thought for a moment as she drew nearer that it was a Blue Magpie which had fallen into the court-yard dead.

She bent forward and saw that it was in fact just a little bunch of single feathers lying on the grass beside one of the flowering bushes.

The as she looked as it she heard a voice whisper:

"Heung Far! Heung Far!"

She started, thinking she must be imagining that someone was calling her. Then incredulously she saw behind a bush against the wall the fingers of a hand beckoning to her.

For a moment she could only stare. The hand seemed to come out of the darkness low down on the ground.

Then the voice, hardly above a whisper, came again:

"Cum, Heung Far! Cum quick!"

Without hesitating Azalea crawled under the bush. The hand was beckoning to her from a hole in the ground that appeared to come from right under the wall.

She crawled forward and the hand retreated.

"Cum! Cum!" the same voice insisted.

Azalea stretched herself forward, her hands in front of her, her body spread out so that she crawled into the darkness that smelt of newly dug earth.

The hole broadened and Azalea realised that she must in fact be in a tunnel that passed right under the high wall of the Convent.

She felt her heart begin to beat quickly with excitement, and although she could not see, she could hear the movements of someone ahead of her.

She must have hesitated, for the hand touched hers and the whisper came again:

"Cum quick! Cum!"

She moved as fast as she could, hampered by the thick folds of her habit and the heavy shoes on her feet.

She put up her hand and, realising that the tunnel was reinforced with wooden supports, she kept her head low.

"Now—storm-water—drain," the whisper came, and Azalea realised that the tunnel had ended and she was in fact inside a large round pipe.

There was only just room enough for her to move her shoulders and she knew that had she been any broader, in fact the size of an average English girl, it would have been impossible for her to follow what she knew was a small Chinese man moving ahead of her.

It was pitch-dark and yet every so often he touched Azalea's hands as if to reassure her that he was there. She knew that he must be crawling backwards down the pipe and she had only to follow him.

It was eerie and rather frightening being so closely confined, but her passage was made easier by the fact that she was descending all the way.

Although sometimes she had to drag herself forward

jerkily because of her skirts, she was still progressing and the incline was growing steeper.

She seemed to have gone a long way, and it was hard to breathe, when Azalea had a moment of panic.

Supposing she suffocated? Supposing she became stuck in this pipe and there was no way out?

She could not go backwards. That was impossible! Ahead there seemed to be no end in sight.

The Chinese who was guiding her did not speak and Azalea thought it must be because their voices would echo and however softly they spoke the sound would be magnified.

There was a pervading smell of rain-water and decaying leaves, and Azalea found herself feeling very hot.

"I cannot breathe!" she longed to cry to her guide.

Then she told herself that there must be air somewhere in the pipes and she must breathe slowly and deeply.

She took one or two deep breaths and moved forward with what seemed fresh impetus.

Quite suddenly she could smell the sea!—what seemed a blessed smell of salt sea-weed, and now it was much easier to breathe!

Then almost before she realised it there was a glimmer of light shining above the dark head of the man in front of her.

At last far away at the end of the pipe she could see daylight! She wanted to cry, then told herself that this was not the moment for weakness.

She was not yet free. Her absence might by now have been discovered. They would find the tunnel, and the Nuns or those they employed could be waiting for her when she finally emerged.

As if her guide also realised the importance of haste he slithered away ahead, moving down the pipe like a snake, and Azalea crawled as quickly as she could after him.

The sunshine was suddenly blinding in her eyes and she saw the shimmer and glimmer of the sea.

She looked out of the storm-water pipe and realised

that it opened in a stone wall high above the waterline of the sea. Below, the Chinese who must have guided her was standing in a sampan.

The man took hold of Azalea's arms and pulled her forward and another man caught her round the waist.

They dragged her clear of the drain and set her down in the sampan.

There was a third man in the bow, his hand on the fixed oar with which the sampan was rowed, and as Azalea seated herself he started moving.

One of the Chinese set a large coolie-hat on her head; another wrapped a wide piece of faded blue cotton round her shoulders.

She knew it was a precaution and a disguise against anyone who might be watching for her from the land. She looked back from under the brim of her hat and saw the Convent, gaunt, grey, and frightening, standing high on the hill above them.

There were few people in sight.

The sampan was rowed past several others and a dozen fishing vessels moored against the sea-wall, and then they were out in the open sea.

It was then that Azalea saw ahead of them a steamship and realised that the sampan was moving towards it.

Her heart leapt with excitement, but as she felt an inexpressible joy she wondered whether a British Captain would feel bound in honour to return her to her Uncle.

Even as the thought came to her she saw that the flag being flown from the steam-ship was not British.

It was Chinese!

It was a large ship and Azalea could hear its engines throbbing as they drew nearer.

There was a rope-ladder hanging over the side, and as she looked at it she knew there was no other way she could climb aboard.

The Chinese in the sampan were smiling as they drew alongside.

"Thank you!" she said in Cantonese. "I am more

grateful than I can ever say! Thank you from the bottom of my heart!"

The two men who had lifted her into the boat bowed.

Azalea knew which one had been her guide in the tunnel and the storm-water drain because his face, hands, and clothes were dirty with earth and she saw as she looked down that her habit was in the same state.

But there was no time to worry about her appearance! She pulled off her coolie-hat and took the blue cotton material from her shoulders.

The two Chinese helped her onto the rope-ladder and she found it difficult in her thick shoes to keep her balance with the sampan moving beneath her, but somehow she managed it, clinging with desperate fingers to the rope as she climbed upwards.

Sailors leant over the side of the ship to assist her aboard.

Without speaking a Naval Officer gesticulated to her to follow him and they walked quickly along the deck.

Azalea knew it was the First-Class deck and after walking for a little way the Officer opened a cabin door.

Azalea entered. Standing inside was Lord Sheldon.

For a moment she could hardly credit that he was there and that she was not dreaming!

Then as the door shut behind her he held out his arms and she ran towards him.

As she hid her face against his shoulder she felt the tears come into her eyes and begin to run down her cheeks.

There was a paean of happiness inside her, but she could not control the tears which seemed for the moment to shake her whole body.

"It is all right, my darling! It is all right! You are safe!"

As Lord Sheldon spoke he undid the veil that she wore over her hair and threw it on the ground.

"I . . . I am . . . so dirty!" Azalea said somewhat incoherently.

"It would not matter to me if you were covered in mud from head to foot!" Lord Sheldon said. "But I know you want to wash and change. You will find, I think, everything you require in the next-door cabin, and then, my darling, we can talk to each other."

She lifted her face to his. The tears were wet on her cheeks and on her long eye-lashes, but her lips were smiling even while they trembled.

"I love you!" he said quietly, then drew her across the cabin to open a door.

"Do not be too long," he added as Azalea closed the door behind her.

The cabin was well furnished in European style, although the designs on the walls were Chinese.

There was a dressing-table fitted to one wall with a large mirror. Azalea looked into it and gave an exclamation of horror.

Her face was dirty and her hands were indescribable. Her habit was covered with earth and dried leaves. The hair-pins had become loosened beneath her veil and her dark hair was trailing over her shoulders.

Quickly, because she could not bear to look at herself, Azalea pulled off the garments she hated and which in themselves had been a penance.

Naked, she went to the washing-stand where she found hot and cold water waiting for her.

The ship had started to move almost as soon as she came aboard and she knew now that they were steaming away from Macao and the prison that she had thought would be hers for life.

When she was clean and had dried herself, Azalea looked round the cabin.

Lord Sheldon had said she would find everything she needed.

Hoping there would be a gown in the wardrobe, she opened it and gave a little gasp of astonishment.

There were three gowns hanging there, one of deep rose-pink with a skirt that swept to the back in frill upon frill of soft crepe ornamented with a big satin bow of the same colour.

Another gown was of jade-green which reminded

her of Mr. Chang's jade treasures, and the third, an evening-gown—the loveliest she had ever seen—was the colour of the Blue Magpie.

There were underclothes, of such fine silk they could have been passed through a ring, which had been embroidered by skilful Chinese fingers to make each garment a work of art.

When Azalea had put them on she arranged her hair and was glad to think that the postulant's veil had prevented it from getting dirty as she had crawled along the pipe.

Then she stepped into the lovely rose-pink gown and found that it fitted her perfectly.

"How could he have known? How could he have guessed?" she wondered.

She thought that perhaps Lord Sheldon had somehow saved from the burning junk the gown she had worn before she had changed into the Chinese garments provided for her by Kai Yin Chang.

When she was ready she stood for a moment, looking at herself in the mirror.

The deep pink of the gown make her skin look like the blossom of a magnolia-tree, and there were blue and purple lights in her hair.

Her eyes were shining like stars and there was an indescribable aura of happiness about her as she opened the door and went back into the cabin.

Lord Sheldon was standing looking out the porthole as Macao faded away into the distance.

He turned round as Azalea entered. Their eyes met and it was impossible for either of them to move.

At last Azalea said a little unsteadily:

"Am I . . . dreaming?"

Lord Sheldon walked towards her and put his arms round her.

"I shall have to convince you that this is real."

"How did you . . . find me? How did you . . . learn where I . . . was?"

He did not answer her question, he merely bent his head and his lips found hers.

She felt a thrill more insistent and more wonderful even than she remembered run through her.

This is what she had dreamt of—this is what she had thought never to know again.

She was safe! She was free!

She loved him so overwhelmingly that she felt as if she became a part of him. Her lips were his and belonged to him like her heart.

Lord Sheldon raised his head and gave a deep sigh.

"I do not think I have ever been so frightened in my life as I have been these past two hours, wondering if I would really get you away, or whether plans would be changed at the last moment and you would not walk in the court-yard as you have done every other day."

"How did you . . . know? How did . . . you find . . . out?"

He smiled and drew her down onto a comfortable sofa.

"We have so much to tell each other," he said, "but let me say first that I love you and that the only thing I want is that we should be married as quickly as possible!"

"How can . . . we do . . . that?"

She felt a sudden tremor of fear that they might be going back to Hong Kong and that Lord Sheldon intended to defy her Uncle.

As if he knew what she was thinking he said quietly:

"We are on our way to Singapore, my darling. We will be married the moment we arrive. I cannot wait any longer to make sure you belong to me!"

"Can we be . . . married?" Azalea asked nervously. "What about my . . . Guardian's . . . permission?"

"The Bishop of Singapore is an old friend," Lord Sheldon answered. "You are an orphan, my precious, and I know when I tell him what has occurred he will only be too willing to marry us."

"But Uncle Frederick . . ." Azalea faltered.

Lord Sheldon smiled.

"Once you are my wife, do you really think that the General will try to interfere or oppose our marriage? On what grounds? Unless he is prepared to state publicly that he does not consider you a suitable bride on account of the secret he has been at such pains to hide."

Azalea felt herself tremble and her fingers tightened on Lord Sheldon's.

"The ... secret ..." she faltered.

"Which is no longer a secret as far as I am concerned," Lord Sheldon said gently. "I know, my precious darling, how your father died."

"How ... could ... you know?" Azalea asked in a low voice.

"I suspected, when you told me he had died of typhoid, that it was not true."

He smiled and added:

"You are not a very convincing liar, my dearest love, and may I say that I am glad about that?"

"B-but how could you ... have found out ... the truth?"

"I think both you and your Uncle forgot that it is very difficult to keep anything secret in India," Lord Sheldon answered. "Travelling with us on the *Orissa* were the wife and children of a Company Sergeant Major of my Regiment."

He paused.

"Their little boy of four and girl of three were among the children you entertained so cleverly during the storm at sea."

"I ... remember ... them," Azalea said.

"Sergeant Major Favel was, I knew, stationed in the same part of India as your father's Regiment. He told me there was a Sepoy in Hong Kong who had served under your father."

Azalea's eyes were raised to Lord Sheldon's as he went on:

"The Sepoy told me how much your father was loved by every man in the Regiment. He informed me that Colonel Stewart's foul behaviour was well known in the Bazaars. He also thought it strange that Major Osmund should have had a shooting accident while hunting a wild animal. He said:

" 'The Major loved animals and I have never known

him to shoot one, however ferocious, all the years I served under him.' "

Azalea made a little inarticulate sound and hid her face against Lord Sheldon's shoulder.

"It was not very difficult, my darling, for me to realise what had happened," he said. "Your father was obviously a very gallant gentleman. And your Uncle had absolutely no right to treat you as he did."

Azalea heard the anger in his voice and raising her head she whispered:

"I still cannot ... believe that I have ... escaped from that ... horrible ... frightening prison!"

"You must not thank me," Lord Sheldon answered, "but Mr. Chang."

"Mr. Chang?"

"It was he who found out that you had been taken to the Convent at Macao and who discovered that one of a gang who had been imprisoned for tunnelling into his warehouse had served his sentence and been released."

"I remembered when I was crawling through the tunnels," Azalea exclaimed, "how Aunt Emily had heard that Chinese robbers had managed to break into the vaults of the Bank and the Merchants' 'go downs' by using the storm-water drains!"

"Mr. Chang was sure it was the only way we could get you away from the Convent," Lord Sheldon said. "The difficulty was to know when you would take exercise, and if you would be alone."

"How did you discover that?"

"No-one noticed a small Chinese boy lying flat on the roof," he replied. "He watched you for two mornings, and we could only pray that you would not have your place of exercise changed, and that you would be alone."

"It was very clever of you!" Azalea cried. "When I heard the Chinese man calling me, I could not believe it was true! How did you remember that 'Heung Far' meant 'Fragrant Flower'?"

"To me you will always typify everything that is

beautiful in a flower," Lord Sheldon answered, his voice deepening. "You were aptly named, my darling, and 'Fragrant flower' is how I shall always think of you. My flower! Mine now and for all time!"

There was a fire behind his eyes and in the deepness of his voice which made Azalea quiver. Then she said:

"Tell me the . . . rest. I have guessed that Kai Yin told you the correct size for my gowns."

"She gave me your dress which was rescued from the fire on board the junk," Lord Sheldon answered. "She helped me to choose the colours which we knew would become you best, and the pure Chinese silk you should always wear next to your skin."

"If you only knew how wonderful it feels after the horrible calico night-gown I had to wear," Azalea said. "It was like an instrument of torture against my back the first night I was in the Convent."

She spoke without thinking, then because of the note of anguish in her voice she saw the look of enquiry in Lord Sheldon's expression, and blushed.

"Why did your back hurt?" he asked.

"U-Uncle Frederick . . . beat me," Azalea replied hesitatingly, "to . . . to make me write . . . that letter to . . . you."

"Damn him! His behaviour is intolerable!" Lord Sheldon ejaculated. "I knew you could not have written it of your own free will, but I did not realise that he would go to such lengths. How could he beat anything so exquisite?"

"I tried to . . . defy him," Azalea said, "but I am a . . . coward."

"You are the bravest person I have ever met," Lord Sheldon contradicted. "I know of no other woman, and I mean this, Azalea, who would have behaved as you did after you were captured by the pirates, or would have been courageous enough to crawl down through that tunnel and down the storm-water pipes as you did today."

He kissed the softness of her cheek before he said:

"All the unhappiness and the misery you have suffered is over. I shall make you happy, my darling, and you shall look as I want you to look—untroubled and unafraid. . . ."

". . . And wildly . . . crazily . . . wonderfully happy!" Azalea finished.

"Do you mean that?" he asked.

"You know I mean it," she answered. "When I was in the Convent I wanted to die . . . but only because I thought I should never see you again."

"I love you as I never thought it possible to love anyone!" he said.

His arm tightened round her.

"We have so many things to do together."

He smiled and added:

"Will it please you to spend part, at any rate, of your honeymoon in India? I have been asked by the Prime Minister to make a report of the various Princely States."

He saw a sudden light in Azalea's eyes and he went on:

"It means staying with a lot of Maharajahs, Governors, and people of importance, but I think we could also get away by ourselves, and I want to see your namesake growing in the foothills of the Himalayas. Would you like that?"

Azalea gave a little cry of joy and put her arms round his neck.

"Everything that I do with you will be marvellous and perfect!" she said. "I was so cold and unhappy in England. It will be like Heaven to be in the sunshine . . . and safe . . . with you!"

"You will always be safe with me," Lord Sheldon said. "That is why, my precious, I am very impatient for this ship to reach Singapore for me to be able to make quite certain that you are my wife!"

His lips were very near to hers and Azalea wanted the touch of them more than she had ever wanted anything in her life.

At the same time, she hesitated.

"Are you . . . sure . . . quite sure . . . that I am really

the person you should marry?" she asked. "You are so important and so clever ... I am afraid of ... failing you."

"You will never do that, my lovely one," he answered, "and there is no question whether you are the right or wrong person. You are mine, all mine! We were made for each other, Azalea, and I think we both knew it that night when I first kissed you in your Uncle's Study."

"It was the most ... wonderful thing that ever happened to me," Azalea whispered.

"And to me," Lord Sheldon answered, "but I assure you, my sweet, it was only the beginning. There is so much more for us to learn; so much more for us to discover about each other. The sort of love that we have found grows and expands until it fills our whole world—yours and mine."

Azalea drew in her breath.

She felt herself vibrate to everything he said and she knew too there was a deep meaning behind his words; something which the Chinese would call "the world behind the world."

For a moment her eyes looked into his, then she said very softly:

"I love you! I will spend all my life ... trying to be as you ... want me to be."

"I love you!" Lord Sheldon answered, "and I will spend all my life making you happy, my darling—my precious fragrant flower, who has always been there in my heart."

He pulled her close and his mouth was on hers.

There was at first something reverent and spiritual in his kiss. Then as he felt her quiver against him, as she drew his head closer to hers, a fire leapt within them both and burned through their bodies, rising until it touched their lips.

It was an ecstasy, a rapture, a joy beyond words. Something so perfect, so miraculous, that it was beyond thought.

It was interwoven with the wonder of the sea, the

blue of the sky, and the glory of the sun on the mountains.

It was theirs and they were a part of it; part of the whole wonder and perfection of love.

ABOUT THE AUTHOR

BARBARA CARTLAND, the celebrated romantic author, historian, playwright, lecturer, political speaker and television personality, has written over 150 books. Miss Cartland has had a number of historical books published and several biographical ones, including that of her brother, Major Ronald Cartland, who was the first Member of Parliament to be killed in the War. This book had a Foreword by Sir Winston Churchill.

In private life, Barbara Cartland, who is a Dame of the Order of St. John of Jerusalem, has fought for better conditions and salaries for Midwives and nurses. As President of the Royal College of Midwives (Hertfordshire Branch), she has been invested with the first Badge of Office ever given in Great Britain, which was subscribed to by the Midwives themselves. She has also championed the cause for old people and founded the first Romany Gypsy Camp in the world.

Barbara Cartland is deeply interested in Vitamin Therapy and is President of the British National Association for Health.